RETURN TO
HOWLIDAY
INN

JAMES HOWE's first book was *Bunnicula*, which has won many awards as a favorite among children throughout the United States and Canada. Howe so enjoyed writing as Harold—the shaggy dog narrator of *Bunnicula*—that he went on to write several other books about Harold and his friends Chester, Howie, and Bunnicula, of which *Return to Howliday Inn* is the latest.

James Howe lives with his wife, Betsy Imershein, and their daughter, Zoe, in Hastings-on-Hudson, New York.

RETURN TO HOWLIDAY INN

JAMES HOWE

Illustrated by Alan Daniel

AN AVON CAMELOT BOOK

AVON BOOKS
A division of
The Hearst Corporation
1350 Avenue of the Americas
New York, New York 10019

Text copyright © 1992 by James Howe
Illustrations copyright © 1992 by Alan Daniel
Published by arrangement with Atheneum, Macmillan Publishing Company
Library of Congress Catalog Card Number: 91-29505
ISBN: 0-380-71972-X
RL: 4.7

First Avon Camelot Printing: March 1993
First Avon Camelot Special Printing: February 1993

CAMELOT TRADEMARK REG. U.S. PAT. OFF. AND IN OTHER COUNTRIES, MARCA REGISTRADA, HECHO EN U.S.A.

Printed in the U.S.A.

OPM 10 9 8 7 6 5

To Zoe

Contents

IT was summer and I was getting ready for a three-day weekend at the shore. Looking around my office for something to read, I picked up a manuscript that had come in earlier that week from one of my authors: *Pickling for Profit and Pleasure*. It was clear a title change would be in order, but that aside it just didn't strike me as beach material. I debated between two other manuscripts—a book by a country veterinarian called *Just a Little Hoarse and What to Do about It* and a seven-hundred-page first novel entitled *Ah, Life!*

Thoroughly discouraged, I told myself I'd pick up a couple of Agatha Christie mysteries at the train station. But then there came a scratching at the door and my weekend reading dilemma was solved.

For there on the other side stood my old friend and valued author, Harold X., an enticing manila envelope gripped between his teeth. Gently, he laid it into my hands and before I could so much as ask if he'd join me for a bowl of cappuccino at the trendy little café that had just opened across the street, he was gone.

With eager anticipation, I opened the envelope and read the letter clipped to his manuscript.

My dear editor and friend,

Enclosed, please find my latest effort. As in the past, it is based on real events from my life and the lives of my family, the Monroes, and my friends, Chester and Howie. Bunnicula was staying with a neighbor at the time these particular episodes occurred. He was fortunate to have been elsewhere, for this was a terrifying adventure indeed. As an old and tired dog, I could well do without such adventures. But as an author, how can I be anything but thankful for them? After all, I doubt your readers would be terribly interested in a mystery called Why Is My Food Dish Empty?

And so, here is the story of my fateful return to the place Chester once dubbed "Howliday Inn." As always, I look forward to your response to my work and, I hope, its eventual publication.

Yours sincerely,
Harold X.

I tucked Harold's manuscript between the sun block and bug spray in my tote bag. I was ready for my weekend—or so I thought.

If only I'd packed a night-light.

ONE

The Omen

IT was the third straight day of rain. The third day of listening to Mr. Monroe whistle the score of *The Phantom of the Opera* through his teeth while indexing his collection of meatless soup recipes. The third day of Mrs. Monroe's saying, increasingly less cheerfully, "Channel Six says it's going to clear by morning." The third day of Pete whining about what a rotten summer it had been and Toby asking When was it going to stop because how could he try his new skateboard? and Were they going to go on vacation even if it kept raining? and Why couldn't they ever rent the movies *he* wanted at the video store?

Not that the Monroes were the only ones getting, shall we say, edgy. No, even we pets—we who ordinarily exemplify a calm acceptance of fate to which humans can merely aspire—even we were losing it. My first inkling of this came when I found Howie racing around the basement on his little dachshund legs going, "Vroom, vroom."

"Uh, Howie, what are you doing?" I asked.

"It's the challenge of my career, Uncle Harold," Howie panted excitedly. "I'm chasing hubcaps at the Indianapolis Five Hundred."

I would have had a little reality chat with Howie then and there if I hadn't caught myself that very morning gazing into the mirror on Mrs. Monroe's closet door and wondering if the time hadn't come for me to try something different with my hair.

Even Bunnicula, usually the calmest of us all, had taken to hopping around his cage as if the floor were covered with hot tar and twitching his nose so rapidly you would have thought he'd suffer from whisker burnout.

Surprisingly, only Chester seemed unaffected by the elements. Or perhaps I should say that if he was affected, it was not in the way one would have anticipated. As the rest of us grew more irritable, Chester mellowed.

"How do you do it?" I moaned on the third night, as the rain continued to pelt the windows and I tried in vain to find an acceptable spot for settling down to sleep. At this point, every square inch of carpet looked the same and I was desperate for a change. Chester, meanwhile, was curled up happily shedding on his favorite brown velvet armchair, an open book in front of him and a contented-on-its-way-to-becoming-smug smile on his face.

"Why aren't you going crazy like everybody else?" I demanded. "What's your secret?"

His smile grew more knowing. "Books," he said, with a nod to the one in front of him, "are not only windows to the world, dear Harold, they are pathways to inner peace."

I shook my head. "I've tried books," I said. "Fifteen minutes and all I ended up with was cardboard breath."

"Try reading them instead of chewing them," Chester advised.

"Oh." This hadn't occurred to me.

Chester is a big reader. The problem is that his reading often gets us into trouble—especially considering the *kinds* of books he likes to read.

"So what are you reading about now?" I asked. "The supernatural?"

"The paranormal," he said.

"Well, that's a relief. Pair of normal what?"

"No, Harold, not a 'pair of normal,' the *paranormal*. How shall I explain this? The paranormal are experiences that are . . . beyond explanation. Like Bunnicula, for example."

Chester believes our little bunny is a vampire.

"Or Howie."

"Howie?"

"I'm still convinced he's part werewolf. That's no ordinary howl on that dog."

[3]

"Uh-huh," I said.

"Or," Chester went on, if I may use the expression with regard to a cat, doggedly, "haven't you ever felt that something was about to happen, you just knew it in your bones, and then, bam! it happened?"

A chill ran down my spine. "Chester!" I cried. "I had a paranormal experience just the other night."

Chester's eyes lit up. "Really? Tell me about it, Harold."

"Well, it was after dinner and I was lying over there by the sofa, where Howie's sleeping now and . . . I was yawning and I felt my eyes growing heavy . . ."

"Yes? Go on."

"And I had this overpowering feeling that I was about to . . ."

"What, Harold? Oh, this is really exciting. Go ahead."

"That I was about to fall asleep. And I did."

Chester looked at me for a long time without speaking. "And do you have the feeling that you're about to experience pain?" he asked at last.

"You mean right now? Well, no."

The book fell off the chair. It landed on my paw. "Ow!" I cried.

"Never discount the paranormal," were Chester's parting words, and he jumped down and headed toward the kitchen in search of a midnight snack.

I wanted to whimper but no one was around or

awake enough to hear. This made me ask myself the question, If a tree falls on a dog in the forest, does the dog make a sound? I was eager to share this provocative conversation starter with Chester when my gaze fell on the open pages at my feet. I began to read.

Harriet M. of Niskayuna, New York, reports the fascinating case of the phantom telephone conversation. *"I had been talking with my sister Shirley for seventeen minutes late one afternoon before I noticed that the phone plug was discon-nected," she writes. "The next day I told Shirley what had happened and when. Stunned, she in-formed me that she had had oral surgery just two hours prior to the phantom conversation and her mouth was wired shut. She would have been incapable of speaking to me even if the phone* had *been hooked up!"*

Incredibly, Harriet herself suffered such ex-treme tooth pain the following day that she too was forced to undergo emergency oral surgery. While under the effects of anesthesia, she re-called her sister's words during their nonexis-tent (??) conversation: "That new dentist is so cute. I'd do anything to see him, wouldn't you?"

"Amazing stuff, isn't it?"
I looked up at the sound of Chester's voice as he emerged from the kitchen, licking milk from his

lips. Now I understood how he'd remained so calm all this time. His brain had turned into a two-week-old banana days ago.

THE rain stopped at exactly three o'clock in the morning. I remember the time because I was awakened just before the clock in the hall chimed the hour. It was not the rain that woke me, however, nor the ticking of the clock. It was a voice.

"Harold," it whispered in my ear, "something terrible is going to happen."

Go away, I thought. But the voice persisted.

"Harold," it intoned. "Wake up."

I knew that voice. Who else would wake me in the middle of the night just to tell me something terrible was going to happen?

"What do you want, Chester?" I mumbled without opening my eyes.

"I've seen an omen." He was louder now that he knew he'd succeeded in awakening me. "Don't you want to see it?"

"That's okay," I said, yawning. "I'll wait for it to come out on video."

"Very funny. Come on, Harold, it's not every day you get to see an omen."

I was going to point out that it was night, not day, but I knew that the difference would be irrelevant to Chester.

Howie was awake now too. He raced over to join us. "I want to see an omen, Pop," he said to Chester. Howie, for unknown reasons, calls Chester "Pop". "What's an omen?"

"A sign that something terrible is going to happen," Chester replied.

Howie shook his head. "I've seen signs like that," he muttered. "NO DOGS ALLOWED. Don't you hate that one? And, oh, here's one that really means something terrible is going to happen: DON'T WALK, when the hydrant is on the other side of the street."

Chester pretended to ignore Howie. "Come on, you two," he said. Apparently, he was unimpressed by the fact that I had both my front paws over my face and was loudly snoring.

"Stop faking, Harold," he said, tapping my eyelids. "Open up. Let's go."

Much against my will, I followed Chester and the relentlessly energetic Howie into the front hall. It was then that the clock struck three and the rain suddenly stopped.

"Look!" Chester commanded. "There, by the front door."

I looked, but I didn't see anything I'd call an omen. I told Chester so.

"Look again," was his response.

And then I saw it.

There, next to the umbrella stand, was Chester's cat carrier. It was open.

"What's that doing there?" I asked.

"And what does it mean?" said Howie.

I felt myself begin to quiver. "It resembles an

open mouth," I sniveled. "It means . . . it means . . . we're all going to have oral surgery! Well, I'm not going! I don't care how cute the dentist is."

"Harold!" Chester snapped. "Nobody's having oral surgery."

"Oh. Well, that's a relief."

"But it does mean we're going somewhere and I don't think we're going to like it."

"Why do you say that?" I asked.

"We would have heard about it if it was anything good. You know what the Monroes are like. They tell us everything. But no one has said a word, so it must be a place too . . . *horrible* . . . to talk about."

There was a scuffling sound in the living room. We turned. Bunnicula was hopping about nervously in his cage. His eyes glistened in the dark.

I ran to him. "Don't worry, little furry friend," I said. "Nothing terrible is going to happen."

"Mark my words," Chester said, "we are doomed."

WHEN I awoke for a second time that morning, I noticed that the sun was shining. I also noticed that Bunnicula was gone.

This wasn't the first time his cage had disappeared without warning and as there had always been a logical explanation in the past, I didn't panic immediately. No, I waited until I heard Mrs. Monroe say, "Good morning, Harold, we have a little surprise for you today."

A fleeting fantasy about chocolate chips in my Mighty Dog aside, I couldn't help thinking that the surprise had something to do with Chester's omen.

Toby bounded into the living room just then, but stopped short when he saw me. His face immediately got what I call its "poor Harold" look. That's when I knew I was in *real* trouble.

He ran over and threw his arms around my neck.

"Don't feel bad, boy," he said. "It's only for a week."

A week? Why did this sound familiar? I looked up at the spot where Bunnicula's cage had been and began to whimper.

"Bunnicula's okay, pal," said Toby. "He's staying with Pete's friend Kyle while we go on vacation. Kyle's dad picked him up real early this morning. *I* said he should go with you and Chester and Howie, but Kyle really, really wanted him to stay with him, so—"

I was out of there and into the kitchen before Toby could finish his sentence.

"Chester!" I cried. "Bunnicula is gone!" Chester barely looked up from his food dish.

"I told you we were doomed," he said in the tone of voice he uses whenever he tells me we're doomed, which is on the average of twice a week.

Howie shook his head. "I can't get any more out of him, Uncle Harold," he said. "He just keeps saying, 'We're doomed, we're doomed.' Oh, and something about 'that place on the hill.' "

"That's it!" I said. "The Monroes are going on vacation and we're going back . . . back to Chateau Bow-Wow."

Howie's eyes were suddenly brimming with tears. "The place of my birth," he sniffed, "my heritage, my roots. Gosh. Uncle Harold, can we take a camera?"

"That would be nice. What do you think, Chester?"

Chester apparently wasn't in the mood to discuss photographic equipment. "I think," he said, "that you both underestimate the seriousness of our predicament. We escaped that dreadful place once, Harold. Will we be so fortunate again?"

I was about to reply when out of the corner of my eye I saw Mr. Monroe coming toward me, my collar in his outstretched hands. "Here you go, Harold, ol' buddy," he said, with a throaty chuckle.

Just as I felt the leather strap tighten around my neck, I heard Chester mutter, "Who knows what new evil awaits us when we return to . . . *Howliday Inn?*"

TWO

Gruel and Unusual Punishment

"HOWLIDAY Inn" was what Chester called Chateau Bow-Wow, the boarding kennel where we'd once spent an eventful week—the very week, in fact, of Howie's birth.

"Aside from your being born there," Chester told Howie as the three of us lurched about in the back of the Monroe's station wagon on the way to our—what had Chester called it again? Oh, yes, our *doom*—"the place is nothing but bad vibes. In the space of one week, Howie, *one week*, there was poisoning, kidnapping, attempted murder, howling in the night—"

"That's not so bad, Pop," Howie said. "Most movies have all that stuff in less than two hours. *And* you have to pay for it!"

"That may be," Chester said, slipping from sight as he lowered himself to the bottom of his carrier, "but this is not a movie, Howie. It's reality."

I wanted to remind Howie that Chester's definition of reality was not necessarily a match for Webster's, but I was feeling a little too carsick at the moment to do anything more than groan.

I groaned the rest of the way to Chateau Bow-Wow.

At first glance, the place looked as I remembered it: a large, creepy house high on a hill with a compound of cages behind it. The compound was surrounded by a tall wooden fence. There was a gate in the fence and a sign on the gate welcoming us. I noticed the sign had been changed. It used to read A SPECIAL BOARDING HOUSE FOR SPECIAL CATS AND DOGS. Now CATS AND DOGS had been replaced by PETS. I wondered at the change. Noticing that change brought other changes to my attention. The house and the cages had been repainted. There were some new shrubs here and there in the compound and the rickety wooden fence had been reinforced by a metal one.

Something more than paint and shrubs was different though. I couldn't put my paw on it, but there was something missing.

Shortly after the Monroes left, Chester, Howie, and I found ourselves standing in the center of the compound in the midday sun. The air was as still as a puppy who's just chewed a hole in the carpet and hears her master's key in the door.

Howie looked around in awe. "So this is where I was born," he said. I followed his gaze as he turned to take it all in. The grassy compound was surrounded on three sides by seemingly empty cages— I made a mental note to tell Howie that at Chateau Bow-Wow "cages" are called "bungalows"—behind which stood the wood-and-metal fence. The fourth wall of the compound was actually the back wall of the house with an extension of fence going out from one corner. There was a door in the wall leading into Dr. Greenbriar's office and a gate in the fence leading outside.

It was incredibly quiet.

"Must be siesta time," Chester quipped.

I nodded in agreement.

Howie sniffed the air. "Maybe we're the only ones here."

That's when it hit me. The big difference in Chateau Bow-Wow was that our friends weren't there. Max, Louise, Georgette, Taxi, Howard and Heather, even crazy Lyle—*they* had been what had made Chateau Bow-Wow so, shall we say, unique. I couldn't imagine the place without them.

A lump was forming in my throat when all at once I heard a familiar voice call out, "Harold! Chester! And oh, my gosh, is that little Howie?"

I turned. There at the door to the office stood Jill,

an old friend. She flung her arms open wide and ran toward us, tripping on a tree root. Another girl followed on the first girl's heels.

Jill gave me a big hug around the neck as I licked her face.

"Do you two know each other?" Howie asked, and he added, "Just a hunch."

"This is Jill," I told him. "She works here. Last time, there was another helper, a real clown named Harrison, but I don't think—"

"Oh, it's so good to see you guys," Jill squealed. "I just got to work and Dr. Greenbriar said you were here. I'm his assistant now, isn't that neat? Of course, Harrison . . . you remember Harrison."

Chester rolled his eyes.

"Well, Harrison has started his own comic book company, so I've taken his job for the summer. And Daisy helps me." She nodded at the other girl.

Daisy looked like a daisy. She had this big, open face and wild, yellow hair. She was also what we pets call a "gusher."

"Ooooo," she crooned, grabbing Howie and squeezing him so tight his eyes bulged, "you are *sooo* cute. I could just eat you up, little puppy.

Howie licked Daisy, which only made her giggle and gush some more. "You're just as cute as the dickens," she said. "How about if I call you Dickens?"

"How about if she calls *me* a cab?" Chester muttered. "I want outta here."

Glancing at the fence, I thought, Not much chance of anybody getting out of this place.

"Daisy," I heard Jill say then, "I'm afraid you're going to have to put Howie down for now."

"Aw, do I have to?"

" 'Fraid so. We really need to finish getting the bungalows ready for these guys."

Daisy nuzzled Howie's nose. "Goodbye, Dickens," she said. "Hug ya later, okay?"

She put Howie gently back on the ground and the two girls walked away. Howie couldn't take his eyes off Daisy. "She's cute," he said with a sigh. "Gee, Uncle Harold, is this what they call puppy love?"

Before I could answer, Chester shook his head and started to walk away. "Dogs," he muttered.

As if on cue, two dogs poked their heads out from behind one of the far bungalows. "Hallo!" shouted the smaller one. "I'm Linda!"

"And I'm Bob!" shouted the other. "Care to join us for a little barbecue?"

BARBECUE-FLAVORED dog biscuits sat propped against the back of what we came to realize was Bob's bungalow. Bob was a cocker spaniel in a Mets cap; his friend Linda was a West Highland white terrier bedecked in a knotted yellow bandanna.

"Don't you just love barbecue?" Linda asked. "Bob and I say we don't know how we get through each winter without it."

"Well, but then there's sushi," said Bob.

I nodded politely. I wasn't aware of any raw fish-flavored dog biscuits on the market, but I kept my ignorance to myself.

"The kids insisted that we be allowed to keep our barbecue biscuits," Linda went on. "That nasty Dr. Greenbriar didn't want to let us. He said something silly about a balanced diet, but the kids told him that *they* were paying the bill and *they* would decide what a balanced diet was."

"Where're you folks from?" Bob asked.

"Centerville," I told him.

"Oh, it's so sweet there," Linda said. "Quaint. Charming. We're from *Upper* Centerville." I could have guessed. "We have a pool. Of course, we have to be careful not to fall in, don't we, Bob?" Bob nodded. "Do you have a pool?"

"We did," Howie said, "until I bit it and the air came out."

Bob and Linda smiled politely as if Howie were just too quaint for words.

"So," Chester said. It was his first word since we'd joined the two dogs. Well, not his first word exactly. He *had* said, "Not if my life depended on it," when they'd asked him if he'd care for a barbecue-flavored dog biscuit. "So," he repeated, "are we *it?* Is anybody else staying here?"

Bob and Linda looked at each other, their brows furrowed.

"Let me put it this way," Bob said at last, "we're the only *normal* ones."

"Really," said Linda. "You won't believe the riff-raff. There are these two cats." She looked at Chester and scrunched up her face as if her dog biscuit had stayed on the barbecue too long. "Trust me," she said. "You don't want to know them. And then there's this character they call 'The Weasel.' "

"Why's that?" Chester asked.

"I expect it's because he's a weasel," said Bob. Turning to Linda, he said, "Don't forget the parrot, hon."

"Oh, that bird!" Linda said, fluttering her eyelashes. "Squawk, squawk, squawk, all day long. Thank heavens they cover it up at night. And then there's this strange dog."

"Size of a horse," said Bob. "And talk about moody. Sheesh. I told him he should lighten up, try deep breathing, get a hobby."

Linda nodded. "Most depressed dog I ever saw," she said. "Oh, if the kids only knew the kind of place they were leaving us."

"This is the longest the kids have been away from us," Bob explained. "They send us postcards, but we can't help but worry."

"Here, let me show you," Linda said. She pulled a card out from behind the biscuit bag. On the front was a picture of a long stretch of sandy beach. On the back were these words:

> *Dear Bob and Linda, Never saw water so blue! Hope you're having fun at Chateau Bow-Wow. We miss you like crazy but need the space. Love, T&T.*

"Tom and Tracy," Linda explained. "The kids."

Chester leaned over and whispered in my ear, "If these two are the normal ones, I can't wait to meet the others."

Linda gasped. "Don't look now," she said, staring at something behind us. Naturally, we all turned to look. Two—what you might call if you were in a forgiving mood—cats were heading in our direction. One, a skinny, striped gray with matted fur, strutted so smoothly her shoulders must have been on ball bearings. Her piercing eyes were stuck on us like hungry fleas. Her blank-faced companion was fat, long-haired, and tabby. As she waddled toward us, I noticed she was chewing something, and I couldn't help wondering how she kept from getting whatever it was stuck in all the long hairs around her mouth.

"Well, well," the gray one snarled as she approached, "and whom have we here, hmm?"

The tabby circled Chester, giving him the once-over. "Nice whiskers," she said in a husky voice when she came full circle. For the first time since I'd known him, Chester appeared to be at a loss for words. The tabby stared him in the eyes and asked, "Did you bring any rations?"

Chester took his time before answering. "Are you talking to me?"

The scrawny gray cat snorted. "Well, she ain't talkin' to yer mother," she cracked, breaking into a snorty sort of laugh. The fat one chortled huskily.

Chester, Howie, and I exchanged nervous glances. Bob and Linda just shook their heads sadly, no doubt wondering what "the kids" would think if only they knew.

The gray cat stopped laughing abruptly. "I'm Felony," she said, spitting out the words. It was less an introduction than a threat. "And this here's my sister, Miss Demeanor."

"You're sisters?" Howie said.

"Sisters in crime," Felony snapped. "Cat burglars. Wanta make somethin' of it?"

There was a long silence during which no one chose to make somethin' of it.

"What were you saying about rations?" Chester asked at last.

Felony sneered. "I'll let you in on a little secret," she said, glancing around. "The glop they serve here is enough to send yer taste buds out on strike."

"They say it's good fer ya," Miss Demeanor chimed in, "but I say so's a flea collar, doesn't mean I want to eat it."

"So we was just wondering if you brought anything widja," Felony went on. "Somethin' besides mosquito-flavored crackers." She snapped a look at Bob and Linda.

"That's 'mesquite,' " Bob said softly.

"Whatever," said Felony, turning back to Chester.

"I'm afraid not," Chester said.

"Pity," said Felony. "You're gonna wish you had."

"The food's that bad?" I asked.

"Like nothin' you ever ate," Felony replied.

"Like nothin' you deserve," said Miss Demeanor.

"Gee," said Howie, "it sounds like gruel and unusual punishment."

Miss Demeanor nodded her head. "However, once Felony and I have found the—," she started to say, but the other cat gave her a sharp look that stopped her cold. Her mouth snapped shut and she resumed chewing.

Chester eyed the two cats suspiciously.

Suddenly, the air was filled with a distant high-pitched voice singing what sounded for all the world like a hymn. The only words I could make out were, "While on the path of righteousness I slither." Felony shook her head in disgust.

"That's The Weasel," she snarled. "A disgrace to his race."

"A shame to his name," said Miss Demeanor.

Howie, who hates being left out, said, "A wart to his sort." We all turned slowly. He smiled up at us and said weakly, "A blot to his lot? A blister to his sister? A bother to his father?"

"Oh, dear," I heard Linda whisper to Bob, "perhaps you and I are the only normal ones here, after all."

I wasn't the only one who heard. "What's that supposed to mean?" Felony said, turning her eyes into tiny slits.

Linda laughed nervously. "Oh, nothing."

"Yeah, well, it better mean nothing. Else, watch out fer yer doggie biscuits."

"Surely," said Bob, arching a superior eyebrow, "stealing dog biscuits is beneath you."

Miss Demeanor arched a superior eyebrow of her own. "*Nothing* is beneath us," she said with pride.

I caught the little smile behind her eyes and began to wonder if Chester might have been right. Perhaps something terrible *was* going to happen.

THREE

Things That Go Bark
in the Night

CHESTER was thinking the same way I was.
"Didn't I tell you?" he muttered, as Jill and
Daisy escorted us to our bungalows. The two of us
trailed behind Jill, while Howie rode first class in
Daisy's arms. "Those two spell trouble."

"I don't know if they're that bright," I said. Per-
sonally, I wasn't sure they were the biggest of our
worries. After all, we hadn't met the hymn-singing
weasel yet.

As it turned out, we didn't have long to wait. He
was staying in the bungalow next to mine.

"Harold," Jill said, "this is The Weasel. Don't let
his name fool you. He's a sweetie, isn't he, Daisy?"

Daisy looked up from where she had her head

buried in Howie's tummy. "I call him Little Dar-
lin'," she said, as if that proved something other
than her own inability to call animals by their
rightful name.

After she and Jill returned to the office, The
Weasel weaseled out of his bungalow and into
mine. I retreated to a corner, not sure how eager I
was for the company of this slinky, not exactly aro-
matic creature with the beady eyes and pointy
nose.

"Hello, friend," he said in a velvety, soothing
tone. I suspect he sensed my discomfort. The fact
that the floor was covered with the hair I'd shed
immediately on his arrival might have been a tip-
off.

"I've just come to spread a little sunshine," he
went on.

"That's nice," I said.

"I just want you to know, since we're going to be
neighbors and all, that you can call on me anytime.
If you need anything, anything at all, I'll be here
as quick as a mink."

"That's very—"

"Weasels get a bum rap, don't you agree?"

"Yes, well—"

"Look at me, do I seem mean, sneaky, homicidal?"

"Gee, I—"

"Of course I don't. Judge not, lest ye be judged,
that's what I always say. Take yourself, for instance." I wanted to take myself right out of there,

but The Weasel was blocking the way. "You're not dumb and lazy and covered with fleas."

"Well, he got one out of three right," I heard Chester crack from the bungalow to my left. I glowered in his direction.

"Would you like to take a stroll with me?" The Weasel asked. "Get acquainted?"

I noticed that he never stopped smiling. I began thinking what a great game-show host he would make.

"Well?" he asked.

"Oh, sorry." I wanted to say no, but fearing that he'd think me lazy if I did, I said, without much conviction, "Sure."

There's one thing I should tell you about Chateau Bow-Wow. For all the fancy security, the bungalows are a snap to open from the inside. We were out in the compound in a flash.

Chester hissed at me as we passed, "Watch your wallet."

"May I come too?" Howie yipped.

"Of course," I said.

It took Howie a minute to maneuver the latch with his nose, and then the three of us set off on our stroll.

After a moment, Howie said, "Wow, to think this is where I was born. I wish my mom and dad were here. What were their names again, Uncle Harold?"

"Howard and Heather."

Howie sighed. "Where was I born, Uncle Harold? I mean, show me the place."

Given the dramatic circumstances surrounding Howie's birth, it wasn't difficult to recall the exact spot. "Over there," I said, nodding toward a far corner of the compound. There wasn't much to see. I instructed Howie to lift his chin.

"Up," I said, "above the fence, on the other side of the compound, what do you see?"

"A roof."

"That's it. That's the roof of the storage shed and inside that storage shed is where you were born."

"Can we go in?"

The Weasel chuckled. "I imagine your parents dug under the fence to get in there, but *nobody* digs under that fence anymore. Believe me, I've tried."

"Aw, shucks," Howie said. He sighed again, deeper this time.

I wanted to ask The Weasel what reason he'd had for trying to dig his way under the fence but a startling sight knocked the question right out of my mind.

A dog, a big dog, the biggest dog I'd ever seen, stood gazing at us with drooping eyes. He woofed once, rather forlornly, then dropped his head as if he'd used up all his energy for the day.

"That's Hamlet," The Weasel informed us. "I visit him at least once a day to cheer him up."

"Why does he need cheering up?" I asked.

"It's a long story. I'll let him tell you," said The

Weasel. Then skittering off ahead of us, he called out, "Hamlet, how are you, my good fellow?"

"I like him," Howie said of The Weasel. "He's really friendly. Besides, it's nice knowing somebody else who looks like a hot dog in a fur coat."

I nodded. I liked The Weasel too, even if he was a little odd. But, then, in my particular circle of friends, who wasn't?

"This is Hamlet," The Weasel said as we approached. "Hamlet, this is Harold and this is Howie."

We both said hello, and Howie asked, "What kind of dog are you, Hamlet?"

"A Dane."

"A Great Dane?" he asked.

"I *was* a Great Dane, but I'm so downhearted these days I don't feel so great anymore."

Howie nodded. "I guess you're more of a melancholy Dane, huh?"

"Indeed," said Hamlet.

"But why?" I asked. "Did something happen to you?"

Hamlet lifted his head enough that he could let it drop again. "In a way," he said. "Accompany me to the community water cooler and I will tell you my sad tale."

As he lumbered slowly ahead of us, I could see his age in every limping step. "Danged arthritis," I heard him mutter.

We all had a drink of water, then Hamlet directed us to a nearby tree. As we gathered around him, he gingerly settled down next to its trunk, cleared his throat, and began to speak.

"I am here because my owner, Archibald Fenster, the great Shakespearean actor—perhaps you've heard of him?" He looked at us in such a hopeful way that I felt sorry to have to shake my head no. In fact, I had no idea what a Shakespearean actor even was, but I didn't want to admit it.

"Ah. Well," said Hamlet and, even sadder now, he went on. "Well, Archie—Archibald Fenster, that is, the great Shakespearean actor—travels a great deal, you see, because he is so in demand. And I have always accompanied him and Little Willie wherever they appeared."

"Little Willie?" I asked.

"His acting partner. They call him that because he's so short. Well, several months ago, Archie informed me that he and Willie were departing on a tour of Europe and that they could not take me with them this time. I was stunned. I whimpered and drooled and panted briskly. But all to no avail.

"He said something about my advanced years and my arthritis, not wanting to put me through the travails of travel and all. But I suspect it was his own advanced years and failing health that made him decide not to take me. I'd probably become a burden to him." Hamlet sighed. "He told me that while he was away, I would stay with his cousin Flo Fenster of Centerville and there he would find me upon his return."

He hesitated long enough to give me a good idea what was coming next. "Three months have passed and Archie has not returned."

"But why are you here?" I asked. "What happened to Cousin Flo?"

"She married a man who loved her dimples but hated her dog," Hamlet replied simply. "I only hope Archie knows where to find me when his journey brings him home at last."

Three months was a long time. I tried to imagine the Monroes being gone for three months. No sharing chocolate treats with Toby. No feeling Mr. Monroe's fingers scratching that special spot between my ears. No surprises in my bowl from Mrs. Monroe. No Pete's smelly socks.

I got choked up just thinking about it. Not the socks, I mean, but the loneliness. No wonder Hamlet was a melancholy Dane.

Just then, a loud raspy voice cried out, *"Dinnertime! Dinnertime!"*

"Sounds like Jill gargled with Drāno," Howie said.

"That isn't Jill, it's Ditto," The Weasel informed us. "Look, there, in the window of Dr. Greenbriar's office."

Far across the compound, just inside Dr. Greenbriar's open window, sat a bird in a cage. A large, green bird with a bent-over beak. *"Din-nertime! Dinnertime!"* it repeated.

"Ditto's great," said The Weasel. "We call her 'the informer.' She's telling us they're going to be out here with our food dishes any minute. We've got to get back to our bungalows before they find us on the loose."

We rose and accompanied the limping, lumbering Hamlet to his bungalow before returning to our own. As he drew closer, he stopped and moaned, "Woe. Oh, woe is me."

"Is the food really that bad?" Howie asked.

"Maybe he's thinking about Archie," I suggested.

"Perhaps it's the cramped quarters," The Weasel said. "Awfully small for such a big dog, don't you think?"

"It's none of the above," said Hamlet. "Rather—" He perked up his ears. "There it is again; don't you hear it?"

I strained to listen, but heard nothing.

"It's coming from over there," said Hamlet. He looked in the direction of the storage shed. And that's when I heard it too. It was a whining, a whimpering sort of sound.

Howie's ears perked up. "Mommy?" he asked. "Is that you?"

"Is there a dog in the shed?" I inquired.

Hamlet shook his head. "That's what I thought when I first heard it. But it seems to be coming from this side of the fence."

Howie ran toward the corner of the compound and began sniffing madly. As we followed, the sound grew louder, although it remained muted, as if it were coming from under something.

"What is it?" I asked.

We all looked to where Howie stood stockstill, his nose pointing toward the ground. Dirt. Nothing but dirt. A chill came over me as I realized that whatever was making the sound was buried beneath the earth.

The whimpering changed to a plaintive barking.

"Wow," Howie said, "I've heard of an underdog, but this is ridiculous!"

Just then, Ditto squawked, *"Get the door, Daisy! Get the door."*

"They're coming!" said The Weasel. "Hurry, back to the bungalows."

As I turned to go, I noticed that Hamlet was shivering. I assumed, considering that it was a hot day and Hamlet's bungalow was only a few yards from where the mysterious noises were emanating, that he shook from fear, not cold.

"Don't worry," I told him. "I'll talk to my friend Chester. He's good at figuring things out."

Wow, I thought, as I raced away with Howie and The Weasel, a real paranormal experience. What would Chester say?

"Baloney!" I heard him mutter as I told him the news over our dinner dishes. A wall separated us,

but I knew Chester well enough to imagine just what his face looked like when he said it.

"What do you mean?" I asked, surprised at his response.

"This food is worse than baloney," he answered. "I can't believe how this place has gone downhill. I'm calling my travel agent when we get home."

I have to admit the food wasn't great, but at least there was lots of it, which is a primary consideration for us canines. Cats, as you undoubtedly know, are much more finicky eaters.

Chester gagged. In cat language, that means the current cuisine has just failed to get a four-star rating.

"Oh, come on," I said, "it isn't *that* bad."

"Speak for yourself," Chester croaked.

On the other side of Chester, Howie piped up, "Hey, Pop! Here's a joke that's right up your alley."

Chester groaned. Howie went on anyway.

"What do you call a fancy dance for rabbits?"

"I give up, Howie. What do you call a fancy dance for rabbits?"

"A hare ball."

Chester hissed. Howie chortled. I tried to get us back on the subject.

"I'm telling you, Chester," I said. "There *was* a sound coming from under the ground. We all heard it."

"Mass hysteria," said Chester. "It's common among dogs."

"I heard it too," The Weasel said from the other side of me.

"If that's your star witness," Chester told me softly, "your case is in serious trouble, Harold."

I was all set to express my astonishment at Chester's failure to be excited by my discovery when the reason dawned on me. It was just because it had been *my* discovery that Chester couldn't get excited. He's usually the one who's onto some mystery or other while I'm home napping. Well, today the tables had been turned and Chester wasn't happy about it. I decided to try a different approach.

"I wish *you* had been there, Chester," I said. "*You* would have known what was going on."

Chester began to purr. "Wellll," he said, "purrrrhaps." I love it when he tries to sound modest.

"Say," I said, "you don't suppose it could be one of those paranormal things, do you, Chester?"

It took a moment for him to reply. "Possibly," he said.

"Maybe a UFO has landed on the other side of the fence."

"These things *do* happen." I could hear the excitement building in his voice. "There are recorded cases. Why, in southern California alone, Harold—"

"Do you think we should investigate?" I asked. I knew if I didn't interrupt he'd be telling me about every UFO sighting he'd ever read about.

"In time, in time," he answered, in a tone that

let me know he thought he was back in charge and he intended to *stay* in charge.

That was okay with me. To tell you the truth, I was just as glad he didn't want to investigate anything at that moment. Full of bad but filling food, I was groggy and ready for a little shut-eye. It wasn't long before I'd fallen fast asleep.

The sound of hushed voices woke me some time later. I'm not sure how much later, but it was dark and the moon was out. I strained to hear.

"No! I've already told you—"

"Come on, be a pal. You're the only one who—"

"Shh, not so loud. You wanna wake up the whole joint?"

I recognized two of the voices as Felony's and Miss Demeanor's, but whose was the third?

"Look, leave me alone, will you? You just don't understand."

"Yeah, yeah, tell it to the judge."

"Listen, we can't do this thing without you."

"And I told you—"

Suddenly, I heard Chester's voice joining the others.

"What's going on out there?" he demanded. That's when I realized the voices were coming from just outside our bungalows.

"Oohh," I heard Miss Demeanor purr. "It's the one with the cute whiskers. How're you doin'? Want some 'nip?"

"Some what?" Chester said.

" 'Nip, 'nip. Want some 'nip to chew? Here."

There was a spitting sound and Chester said, "Good grief, I don't want your used catnip."

I moved to the front of my bungalow and looked out. Miss Demeanor was retrieving something from the ground. "I prefer to think of it as sharing," she muttered.

Chester sighed. "That is so gross," he said. "But you didn't answer my question. What's going on out there?"

"Just gettin' a little air," said Felony, coming into view. "What's it to ya?"

"It sounded to me like you were scheming something."

"We're always scheming something," said Felony. "We're cats."

Chester didn't have an argument for that one.

Just then, Linda's voice rang out in the night air, "But, Bob, we can't just do *nothing*. We *must* find out what's happened to them!"

Before Bob or anyone else had a chance to react, there came a second voice: tiny, plaintive, and so out-and-out weird that it sent a shiver of fear through every part of me.

At first it barked. Then it began to cry out in a strangled sort of way, "Let me out! Please . . . let . . . me . . . out . . . of . . . here!"

FOUR

Rosebud

"AH-OOOOOOOOOOOO!" Howie's frightened howl—the kind Chester likes to describe as werewolvian—seemed to make the very walls of our bungalows quiver and shake.

As fast as we could, we unlatched our doors and hurried across the compound, where we gathered in a hushed semicircle around that curious mound of dirt. I glanced to my left. Bob and Linda were huddled together, their teeth rattling. Next to them were the two cat burglars, looking a little more like timid pussycats than they might have wished. To my right, The Weasel was softly singing an inspirational tune in a tremulous voice while Hamlet whimpered and Howie woofed.

Chester, meanwhile, stared unwaveringly at the

mound of dirt, his head thrust forward in the classic feline stalking position or, as he prefers to call it, his don't-make-a-move-I've-got-you-covered look.

"What do you think?" I whispered.

"I think there's someone in there," he said.

At that, the general level of rattling, whimpering, and woofing rose sharply and The Weasel burst out singing: "I will be brave, I will be strong, I will be right, unless I am wrong."

If this was some sort of weasel anthem, it was pretty wishy-washy. No one bothered to comment, however. We were all much too busy listening to our own hearts thumping wildly in our chests.

"Let me out!" called the voice from beneath the ground.

"Oh, Bob," I heard Linda say, "why couldn't they have gone to a Club Med and taken us with them?"

"I don't know about anybody else," said Chester, "but I think it's time we did a little digging. Harold."

"What?"

"You're a good digger. I've seen you."

"Why is it you only compliment me when you want something?" I asked.

Chester turned, a surprised look on his face. "That isn't true. Just the other day, I told you I liked your eyes."

"Yes, but when I got up to look in the mirror, you took my spot on the rug."

"Would you two get on with it?" the voice in the

ground snapped. "You sound like an old married couple."

Chester and I looked at each other. This was getting weirder by the minute. I asked Howie to help me and we began to dig.

It didn't take long before we'd found something suspicious.

Bones. Small, white, dry bones.

The others gasped as Howie and I laid them out in a line on the ground. Then Howie noticed something else, a pinkish something studded with shining stones that glittered in the moonlight.

Howie extracted it carefully with his teeth and dropped it at Chester's feet.

"What do you make of it?" I asked.

"It's a collar," Chester said. The crowd bandied the word about in amazed whispers as Chester struggled to read the dirt-smudged gold letters embossed on the side.

"R-O-S-E-B-U-D," he read. "Rosebud."

"But what does it mean?" I asked.

Chester began to pant, a sign that he was either very excited or dehydrated. The fact that he didn't ask for a glass of water led me to believe it was the former.

"This is incredible!" he exclaimed. "Harold, we're having a real paranormal experience here."

"Are you sure it's not mass hysteria?"

Chester gave me a cool look, which was no mean trick considering he was still panting. "Cats don't participate in mass hysteria, Harold. If we're going to be hysterical, we do it on our own. We're individuals, not groupies like you canines. No, this is the real thing. Talking bones! And Rosebud! Rosebud, Harold!"

"But what does it mean?" I asked again.

"It was my name," said the voice.

Howie was a couple of feet away from me, but I could feel him trembling as he whimpered, "I want to go home, Uncle Harold. I don't want to stay in a place where bones and collars talk."

"I am not a talking collar," said the voice. "I am the spirit of Rosebud. These are my bones. In life I was a Yorkshire terrier."

"Good heavens!" Hamlet exclaimed.

"What is it?" I asked.

He turned his anguished face to me. "Alas, poor Yorkie," he said. "I knew her, Harold."

"You did?"

"She was being boarded here when I first came. She was supposed to stay seven days, but on the morning of the fourth day she was gone. We all assumed her owners had come for her during the night. But apparently . . ."

Chester nodded his head slowly. "Apparently, she met with foul play," he said.

"Foul play?" The Weasel repeated. "Surely you don't mean—"

"Murder," said Chester. I gulped. Chester had said the same thing the last time we stayed at Chateau Bow-Wow and had been so far off base he may as well have been in a different ballpark. But this time, the evidence was right before our eyes.

"Murrr-der," Rosebud echoed eerily. "Murrr-der."

Chester inched his way toward the talking bones. "But why?" he asked. "Why were you murdered?"

It took a moment before the voice spoke again. "Because . . . I stumbled upon . . . the truth."

A cold wind blew. No one dared to speak. No one, that is, but a pile of bones and a worn pink collar named Rosebud.

"It happened one morning when the door to the office had been left open by mistake. Curious, I followed my nose in and poked about, hoping to find something good to eat."

I noticed Felony and Miss Demeanor nod appreciatively.

"One door was locked," Rosebud went on, "but another door—a door at the end of a hall—was open just a crack. This was the door that led to my demise. When I pushed it open, I sealed my fate."

She stopped to clear her throat, which was more than a little bizarre, since she didn't have a throat that I could see.

"Be warned," she said when she resumed, her voice now full of fear and foreboding. "None of you is safe! Get out while you can, *escape* . . . before the secret of Chateau Bow-Wow does to you what it did to me."

"But, um, excuse me," The Weasel said, "I don't

mean to interrupt Your Ghostiness, but if we stay
out of the office, away from that forbidden door,
how can we get in trouble?"

There was a long pause. And then: "The secret
is bigger than the place that contains it. If you do
not find it, it may find you. Escape, all of you, before it is too late."

"But—," Chester said.

The voice, faint now, fading into the darkness
of the night, cut him off. "Remember me," it said,
"Rosebud, the blossom that never opened. The terminated terrier. Remember me, remember me."

"But, wait," Chester said, "the secret of Chateau
Bow-Wow, why can't you just tell us what it was?"

"There is . . ."

We all moved in to listen. The voice was so tiny
now we could barely make out the words.

"There is a—"

"What is going on out here?" a new voice
thundered.

Terrified, we turned. There in the doorway to the
office stood a giant of a man. A beam of light
stretched out from his hand and caught us all in it
like a net.

I swallowed hard as the man began walking
slowly toward us.

"On the whole," I said to Chester, "I think I
might have preferred oral surgery."

The giant, it turned out, was none other than Dr.
Greenbriar. And while his anger was great, the rest

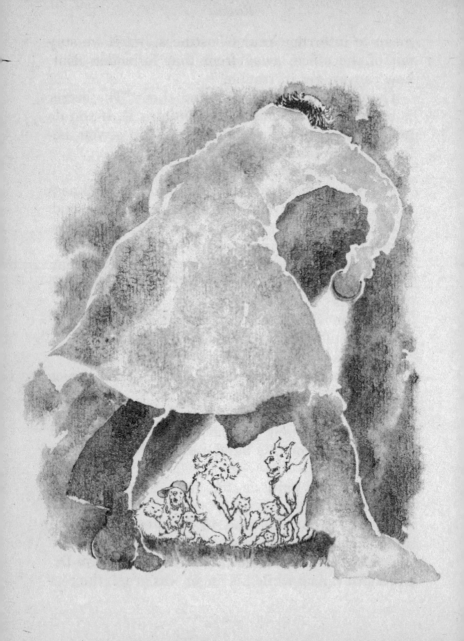

of him was no bigger than usual. He had seemed like a giant only because of the way his shadow fell from the doorway.

"I don't understand it," he mumbled as he rounded us all up and returned us to our bungalows. Howie, thinking quickly, had covered Rosebud's bones and collar with loose dirt. "How do you fellas keep getting out? I think it must be Daisy. She's such a scatterbrain. I'm going to have to speak to Jill about her. Oh, what a nuisance!"

He sighed and it grew into a yawn. What was he doing here in the middle of the night anyway?

From our bungalows we watched him retreat into his office. The light stayed on for a long time. I don't know about anybody else, but I was wishing Ditto's blanket were off so she could report on what was happening in there.

"Psst."

I looked up. The Weasel was outside my cage. "Meeting at Hamlet's when the light goes out," he whispered. He scurried off and I heard him repeat the message to Howie and Chester and then watched him slither across to the bungalows opposite to tell the others.

I began thinking about everything that had just happened. Talking bones, secrets, murder, escape. Boy, I thought, why couldn't the Monroes send us to a place with normal social activities? Volleyball, maybe, or bingo.

"Chester," I called softly through the wall of my bungalow.

"Yes, Harold?"

"What do you think?"

There was a pause before Chester spoke again. "I think we are in danger, Harold, that's what I think. Until we discover the secret of Chateau Bow-Wow, no one here is safe. Any one of us could wake up like Rosebud, nothing but a pile of bones. So whatever you do, stay awake, Harold. Stay awake, keep alert, be ever vigilant because . . ."

I don't remember the rest of what Chester had to say. I had fallen into a deep sleep.

FIVE

The Meeting

IWAS jarred awake by Chester's rattling the door of my bungalow. "What are you doing out there?" I asked.

"I came to *wake* you," he said pointedly. "We have a meeting, remember?" He nodded toward the office; the light was out. "Dr. Greenbriar left a few minutes ago. Come on, Harold, shake a leg."

I yawned and slouched toward the door. It was the middle of the night and I was hungry. I wondered if they'd be serving doughnuts at this meeting.

Howie was waiting outside with Chester. We started toward Hamlet's bungalow.

"Boy, this is exciting, huh, Uncle Harold? I've never been to a meeting before. Do you think we'll get to vote? I hope so. I've always wanted to say, 'I abstain!' Do you want to hear my speech?"

"Your what?"

"My speech. In case I get nominated for office."

Chester and I exchanged glances.

"I don't think—," Chester started to say.

"If elected," Howie burst out earnestly, "I promise to get the job done first and talk about it later. The buck stops here, a chicken in every pot, Motherhood, America, and do you know where your kids are? Sure, my opponent accuses me of drooling on hot summer days. Well, you know what I say to that? I say, Show me a dog who doesn't drool on hot summer days and I'll show you a hypocrite! I have videotaped evidence of my opponent drooling in the luxury of his own air-conditioned doghouse just this past July and I am willing to go nose to nose anytime, anywhere—"

"Howie," Chester interjected, "I don't believe there are going to be any elections at this meeting."

"Oh," Howie said. "Well, maybe I could be sergeant at arms."

Fortunately, we arrived at Hamlet's bungalow before the discussion could go much further. The others were already there.

"I move the meeting be adjourned!" Howie cried as we gathered in a circle.

"Ignore him," Chester advised the others.

Taking Chester's advice, Hamlet spoke up. "I'm

sorry to say it, but I'm kind of relieved this happened. I've been hearing this whimpering and moaning for a few days now and I was beginning to think I'd lost my marbles."

"Well, now we've all heard it," said Chester. "So either we've all lost our marbles, or what we heard, difficult as it may be to accept with a rational mind, is as real as any of us sitting here."

"Oh, we heard it all right," said Linda.

"But what are we going to do?" Bob asked. "We have to escape, but how?"

"Well," said Linda, as if the two of them were having a private conversation, "why couldn't we dig our way out, Bob?" Then, turning to the rest of us, she said, "Unfortunately, the kids have us so well trained that we have very little personal digging experience and they have a gardener who does most of their digging, so I can't even say we've seen it done."

"The Great Escape," Bob said.

"Sorry?" said Linda.

"We saw a lot of digging in that movie, *The Great Escape,* remember, hon? Tom and Tracy rented it the night Shelly and Chad came over. You got sick from the popcorn after."

"Of course," Linda said. "Well, there you are. We *do* know a thing or two about digging. Perhaps we could act as technical consultants."

At this point, even Howie looked confused.

"On the subject of digging," said The Weasel,

"I have to point out that the metal fence goes a long way down. I don't want to be discouraging, but—"

"What about the gate?" Chester asked. "Or the office? Isn't there some other way out?"

Felony and Miss Demeanor looked at each other knowingly, an exchange that was not lost on Chester.

"You know what we're talkin' here, pal?" Felony asked. Chester shook his head. "Max seck."

"Who's Max Seck?" Chester asked.

"Maximum security," said Miss Demeanor, still chomping on her catnip.

"I . . . I hate to mention it," Hamlet said haltingly. "But Rosebud did seem to imply some urgency. Perhaps some of us should start digging while others work on figuring out a different escape plan."

"Done!" Chester snapped. "Dogs dig; cats figure."

"Where do I fit in?" The Weasel asked before the dogs among us had a chance to form a union and go on strike.

"That's a question I've been asking myself ever since I met you," Chester said. "You can dig, but you might also be useful getting into tight places— such as the office, for instance."

The Weasel ran his tongue nervously along his lips. "I know it's important that we get out, but, um, what if we get caught?"

"Aw, stop bein' such a goody four-paws," said Felony, with a disdainful sneer. The Weasel looked away, embarrassed.

"Excuse me," said Hamlet, inching his right front paw forward on the ground. "I don't know how much help I'll be with the digging. My leg isn't so good. Danged arthritis. I'm sorry."

We all nodded sympathetically.

"That's all right," said Chester. "We'll figure out something for you to do. Which reminds me: the parrot."

"Ditto," said Howie.

Chester gave Howie an irritated glance. "Maybe there's some way he can help out."

"She," said The Weasel.

"Ditto," Howie said.

"What?" said Chester.

"The parrot is a she," The Weasel pointed out.

"Ditto," Howie repeated.

Chester said, "Howie, would you stop that? If you have something to say, at least be original."

"The parrot's name is Ditto," said Howie.

"Well, of course it is!" Chester shouted. He grabbed his tail and began licking it with all his might. I've seen this before. It's his watch-me-do-this-and-maybe-you'll-forget-what-a-fool-I-just-made-of-myself ploy.

"Look," Linda said, "there's a shrub in front of the fence between Felony's and Miss Demeanor's bungalows. Perhaps we could dig a hole behind that. That way, it would be hidden from view."

"Good thinking," Chester said. "Okay, so the dogs will dig. And the cats, with Ditto's help, will try to figure out a way to break into the office or unlock the gate. Is everyone agreed?"

"Let's vote!" Howie cried.

"We don't need to vote," said Chester.

"Please, Pop!"

"Howie," Chester said, "go work on your acceptance speech."

Howie looked startled. "You mean I won?" he asked. "Wow, and to think I never even kissed a baby or threw mud at my opponent. I was looking forward to that part." And he trotted off.

"I been thinkin'," Felony piped up. "It's kinda strange we ain't heard nothin' from the bones this whole time."

"Do you mean Rosebud?" I asked.

"Yeah, yeah, Rosebones. What do you say we ask her some questions? Like, fr'instance, What is the secret of Chateau Bow-Wow? She was about to spill the beans just before old Doc Greenbriar appeared on the scene."

"Maybe the secret's got somethin' to do with him," Miss Demeanor said. "Maybe that's why he was here tonight. He knew somethin' was up and he was spyin' on us."

"Maybe there are more bones buried around the place," said The Weasel.

"You don't mean to suggest," said Hamlet, "that there were others before Rosebud, others who . . . never went home?"

A shiver went through me.

"What're we waitin' fer?" Felony piped up. "Let's go ask her."

We all crept over to the spot where Howie had hastily covered the remains of Rosebud. Chester called to her softly. She didn't answer. He tried again. And again.

"Perhaps she's on another plane of existence," Hamlet suggested, "and she can't hear us right now."

"Well, they ought to have answering machines on the Other Side," Linda said, "so if they're tied up on another plane of existence, you could just leave a message at the beep."

"Great idea, hon," said Bob.

The Weasel suggested we try again in the morning.

"Right," I said with a loud yawn. "Nothing's going to happen between now and breakfast."

"I'm not sure I agree with you," Chester remarked as we walked back to our bungalows. "Anything can happen, Harold. And it can happen anytime. It's true we must escape, but the only way we're going to be safe, really safe, is for someone to find out the secret of Chateau Bow-Wow. If it isn't going to be Rosebud, then it will take someone else, someone heroic, someone who dares to go where no one has gone before, someone who is willing to risk life and limb—"

"Wait a minute, Chester," I said. "If you think you're going to flatter me into this . . ."

"I was referring to myself," Chester said flatly. "*I'm* going to find out the secret of Chateau Bow-Wow, Harold."

I turned to face him. His eyes were filled with determination. I knew there was no swaying him, no matter what terrible fate might lie in store. A shiver of dread went through me.

Even as I tried to fall asleep, I couldn't shake the chill. Nor could I shake Howie's ranting two bungalows away:

"I will not shirk my responsibilities nor forget the promises I made on my way to being elected. More miles to the gallon, more crunch in every spoonful, and a par-tri-idge in a . . . pear . . . tree."

SIX

The Secret of Chateau Bow-Wow

MORNING exercise is not my favorite thing in the world. Let me put it another way: My idea of morning exercise is raising one eyelid followed within the hour by the raising of the second eyelid. If I'm feeling really ambitious, I sometimes roll over.

When I raised both eyelids this particular morning, I saw that rolling over wasn't going to cut the mustard at Chateau Bow-Wow. There in the center of the compound were Daisy and Jill wearing identical warm-up suits. I know they're called that because Mr. and Mrs. Monroe have similar ones, except that unlike Daisy's and Jill's they don't say

WE'RE ANIMALS FOR EXERCISE on the front and A PHYSICALLY FIT PET IS A HAPPY PET on the back.

"Okay, everybody!" Jill shouted, as she bounced up and down. "It's aerobics time!"

The silence was deafening.

Daisy ran around, throwing open all our cages and crooning, "Out you go, little cuties, nothing like a little workout before breakfast!"

Only Howie exhibited enthusiasm and that's because he's a puppy and doesn't know any better.

Chester and I joined the others in a circle run. I heard him mumbling something about calling his lawyer after he'd called his travel agent just as soon as he got home. At one point, we passed Felony and Miss Demeanor, who clammed up the moment they spotted us. What were those two up to anyway?

Chester was curious too. So he informed me after breakfast (a curious dish that had the consistency of a paste-and-kitty-litter pudding), although not until he'd had the chance to offer commentary on my dining habits.

"How can you eat that slop?" he asked, eyeing my empty bowl. I noticed he hadn't touched his.

"I pretended it was a hot fudge sundae," I said, a hair defensively. "Don't you ever use your imagination?" I realized the moment these words left my mouth that asking this of Chester was a little like asking a dancer if he ever used his feet.

Chester rolled his eyes and sighed.

"If I may change the subject," he began.

"*You* brought up breakfast," I said.

"Nice turn of phrase, Harold." Clearing his throat, he went on, "Have you noticed anything odd about those two cats?" He indicated Felony and Miss Demeanor, who were stretched out in a patch of sun in front of their bungalows. Felony was twitching her head this way and that, either trying to keep up with a fly or auditioning for the part of Robocat. Miss Demeanor lay flat on her stomach like an imitation bear rug. Her head bobbed up and down to the rhythm of her chewing.

"No," I said, "they seem like normal cats to me."

"They are definitely up to something," Chester said. "I wonder if they have something to do with the secret of Chateau Bow-Wow. I know one way for us to find out."

"What's that?"

"You."

"Excuse me?"

"I want you to pal around with them, Harold. When you're not busy digging our tunnel to freedom, that is."

I started to protest, but Chester was already way ahead of me. "It'll be easy. You're going to be hanging out on their turf anyway. Just see if you can get them to leak some information."

"What are you going to be doing, if you don't mind my asking, while I'm looking for leaks?"

He lifted his head and stared off toward the office. "I'm going inside," he said dramatically.

"Ah." I looked over at the office window. Through it, I could see Ditto pecking at some birdseed in her cage. Beyond her, there was a general bustle and commotion as Daisy, Jill, and Dr. Greenbriar went about their business.

"And exactly how do you think you're going to get in there, Chester?" I asked. "It's not like you have an appointment."

"True. But I do have charm," said Chester.

I cocked an eyebrow at this one.

"And if all else fails, there's the bird. A veritable font of information."

An hour later, Chester found me digging behind the bush between Felony's and Miss Demeanor's bungalows.

"What did you find out?" I asked.

"That charm without an appointment only gets you as far as the door. And Polly wants a cracker."

I nodded. Chester looked at the hole. It wasn't very impressive, but then again we hadn't been digging very long. Howie was still on a break that had begun a few minutes after we'd started; he was at Bob and Linda's having smoked Gouda—flavored doggie bones. The Weasel and Hamlet were trying to see if they could get Rosebud talking again. And as for the cat burglars . . .

"What did *you* find out?" Chester asked.

"Talk about forthcoming," I said. "I kept track of

their answers. There were four 'What's it to ya's,'
three 'What d'ya wanna know for's,' seven 'Mind
yer own business's,' and one, 'What're you, a police
dog?' "

"Gosh," said Chester, "what kind of questions did
you ask?"

"Nine out of fifteen were about the weather."

Chester shook his head. "Where are they now?"

I shrugged. "Looking for trouble or making it," I
said. "They didn't let me in on their plans."

"Hmm," said Chester, looking decidedly un-
happy, "this is going to be a lot tougher than I
thought. Let's see how Hamlet and The Weasel are
doing."

I was pleased to stop digging. Not even halfway
through the job and I was already wondering if I'd
ever get the dirt out from under my nails. Lucky
Hamlet, I thought, not to have to dig at all. But
when I saw his woebegone face and remembered
his limp, I decided maybe he wasn't so lucky after
all.

The Weasel looked up from where he and Hamlet
were hunched over what I presumed were Rosebud's remains and headed toward us like an express train. He was out of breath when he
announced, "She spoke to us. Oh, dear, oh, dear."

"Calm down," said Chester. "Come on, take a
breath."

The Weasel sucked in air with such force I felt
my whiskers tingle. "Oh, my, oh, dear, oh, my,"

he exclaimed as he exhaled. "This is terrible, just awful."

"What?" I asked, not sure I wanted to know.

"You tell them, Hamlet," The Weasel said as we approached the woeful Dane. "I can't, I just can't say the words."

"It was a warning," Hamlet told us. "We asked her about the secret. She wouldn't talk at first. Then, when she did, it was more a riddle than an answer. 'My fate is a mirror in which to see.' "

"Th-there was more," The Weasel panted. " 'One will look in and end like me.' "

Chester nodded slowly as he repeated the words. "My fate is a mirror in which to see. One will look in and end like me." He looked off toward the office. Through the window, it appeared that Ditto was alone.

"This is my chance," Chester said. "Maybe I can get her to talk."

"But, Chester," I said, "the warning."

He was halfway across the compound before I could get out the rest. "What if Rosebud means *you?*"

CHESTER was gone for most of the afternoon. I spent the time digging. It went very slowly. Bob and Linda were more talk than action. Howie and The Weasel had small paws. I was getting more worn-out by the minute.

And the metal fence seemed to have no bottom.

It was late in the day before Chester returned, a jubilant expression on his face. I looked up as he jerked his head toward our bungalows. Howie and I ran to join him.

"Nice of you to show up," I said. "Don't tell me you've spent this whole time talking crackers with a parrot?"

"Oh, we had a much more interesting conversation than that," Chester exclaimed. He looked around and lowered his voice. "I've learned the secret of Chateau Bow-Wow!"

"Really?"

"Wow," said Howie.

"It's a code, so I still have my work cut out for me."

"Is it a common code?" Howie asked. "Or more of a flu?"

"It's a number code," said Chester, gritting his teeth. "All I have to do is make sense of it. For a while there, I thought I wasn't going to get anything out of her, then all of a sudden she started repeating these numbers. Over and over. It has to mean something, don't you see?"

He looked around to be sure no one was listening, leaned his head in toward ours, and said very softly, "Six-one-one-one-five."

"Six-one-one-one-five?" Howie yelled excitedly.

"Howie!" said Chester, annoyed.

"That's it!" someone shouted.

"Ee-yes!"

We looked up. Felony and Miss Demeanor smiled down at us from atop Chester's bungalow, then scampered off.

"Nice going," Chester told Howie.

Howie lowered his head and looked up at Chester sheepishly.

"I'm sorry, Pop," he said. "I get carried away."

"Don't tempt me," said Chester. "Now where are those two off to? And why did they want to know the code? I'm telling you, Harold, those two are our culprits. I'm going to follow them and you can—"

Chester was cut off by Ditto's sudden squawking. *"New one coming tonight! New one coming tonight! Hamlet got to go! Hamlet got to go!"*

I looked around. Bob and Linda were sitting on their haunches in front of their bungalow, staring wide-eyed at the jabbering bird. Felony and Miss Demeanor had stopped in their tracks halfway between our bungalows and theirs. They too were staring. The Weasel's head poked out from behind the bush. He turned sharply. I followed the direction of his gaze.

He was looking at Hamlet, who was quivering with fear.

"Too late!" cried Rosebud. "Too late!"

The door to the office opened. Daisy came out and walked slowly the full length of the compound. Reaching Hamlet, she burst into tears. "I'm sorry," she said, sniffling. "I'm so sorry." She put her arms

around his neck and hugged him for a long time. Then she took hold of his collar and led him away.

As he reached the office door, Hamlet turned back and looked at us. He raised his head and let out a piteous whimper, one that filled the very air with sadness and left it empty as the sound died away.

"The rest is silence," he said.

Daisy tugged gently on his collar. They walked into the office. The door closed.

And the rest was silence.

SEVEN

A New Arrival

SILENCE remained like an unwanted guest.
The only thing that broke it was Chester's mut-
tering from the next bungalow after dinner. Numbers, letters—I knew what he was up to. He was
trying to decipher the code.

After Hamlet's departure, although no one had
said as much, it was clear we were all thinking the
same thing: Something terrible was going to happen to him. Chester was convinced that the answer
lay in the code, which was going to reveal the secret of Chateau Bow-Wow and somehow help us
understand Hamlet's fate.

As it turned out, it wasn't the code that helped
us so much as a ditsy little poodle who arrived later
that night.

But I'm getting ahead of myself.

It was just beginning to get dark when Chester cried, "Harold!"

"What is it?!" I was so startled I bumped my nose on the wall as I swung around to face Chester's bungalow.

"I've got it," he whispered hoarsely. "I'm coming over."

A moment later, he was inside my bungalow.

"I've been substituting letters for numbers. It took me a while to get the right combination, but now I have it, I'm sure of it. Six, one, one, one, five. Six equals *F*. That's easy."

"If you say so," I said.

"One is *A*, the next two ones are eleven, that equals *K*, and the five means *E*. Put them all together, they spell—"

"Muh-uh-uhther!" I sang out. I'm a sucker for that song.

"Knock it off, Harold," Chester snapped. "It spells *fake*. Get it?"

"No," I said. "Fake what?"

"I don't know that yet. Maybe Greenbriar's a fake. Maybe he forges documents, makes counterfeit money in the cellar. Whatever it is, my guess is that Chateau Bow-Wow is nothing but a cover for some sleazy, shady operation. Rosebud must have found out. And then Hamlet."

I gulped. "And now you."

"Correction," he said, "now *us*."

I gulped again. This time it stuck in my throat.

Dashing to the door, Chester said, "Excuse me, Harold, but I've got some bones to talk to."

And he was gone.

How like a cat. They stop by long enough to tell you you're a dead dog, then rush off to talk to an even deader one.

Well, I wasn't about to spend my evening sitting around worrying what terrible fate lay in store. No, I would figure some things out myself.

I sat down and began to think.

Fake.

What did it mean?

After several seconds, my head started to hurt from thinking and I was getting nowhere. I decided to drop in on Howie. Maybe if he did half the thinking my head would hurt only half as much.

I told him what Chester had told me.

"Do you think Dr. Greenbriar is a quack?" I asked him.

"You mean a vet who specializes in ducks?" Howie said. "That's what I call a fowl practice. Get it, Uncle Harold, get it? A *fowl* practice."

For some reason, my head began hurting more instead of less.

"A quack is a doctor who doesn't have a license, a phony. If Dr. Greenbriar is found out to be a quack, he could go to jail."

"That would be terrible," Howie said. "There aren't any ducks in jail. Who would he take care of?"

I had the feeling I'd lost Howie.

Just then, Chester appeared at the door of Howie's bungalow. "Harold, Howie," he said, "hard as it is for me to admit this, I need you."

Howie scampered over to Chester. "Aw, Pop," he said, "we need you too, don't we, Uncle Harold?"

The Weasel suddenly popped up next to Chester. "I couldn't help overhearing and if you don't mind my saying so it's about time you three lovable guys told each other how much you cared. What a beautiful moment. There's a little song I could sing—"

"Rosebud's not talking," said Chester, not giving The Weasel a chance to finish his sentence, let alone break into song. "I thought maybe she'd talk to a dog. Harold?"

"I'll try," I said.

"Me too," cried Howie.

"I'll sing backup," said The Weasel.

And off we went.

It was no good. A half hour of calling Rosebud's name, of asking her the meaning of the word *fake*, of telling her what happened to Hamlet—all to no avail. She was as silent as, well, as silent as a bunch of bones and an old collar.

"Here, Georgette, here, girl! Here, Georgette, that's a girl!"

We all turned toward the office window. The light had come on and Ditto was squawking in her cage.

"Here, Georgette, out we go!"

"Georgette," Chester said under his breath. "Surely not—"

"We'd better get back," said The Weasel. "Someone's coming."

Just before we hurried off to our bungalows, I heard a female voice behind me say, "Someone's coming. Maybe this will be our chance." I glanced over my shoulder. In the darkness, I couldn't tell if it was one of the cat burglars who had uttered those words or Linda talking to Bob.

Once inside our bungalows, I whispered through the wall to Chester, "Did you hear that?"

"Very interesting," he said.

In the distance, the office door clicked open.

"Very interesting," Chester repeated softly.

There in silhouette stood Jill with a leash in her hand, at the end of which was a small, curly-haired dog. A poodle. The aroma of lilac and honeysuckle wafted through the air.

Her name was Georgette.

"Harold!" she cried as she spotted me on her way to Hamlet's former bungalow. "What're y'all doin' here?"

"The usual," I said. "Solving mysteries. Talking to bones. Fearing for my life."

Georgette giggled. "You're such a tease," she said. "We'll talk later, okay?"

"Okay," I said.

"Who was that?" I heard Howie ask Chester.

"Her name's Georgette," Chester answered. "She was boarded here the last time we were."

As Jill helped Georgette settle into her bungalow, I heard a soft rustling sound and caught a blur of movement across the way. Bob's door was slightly ajar; his bungalow was dark.

"He's gone," I murmured.

He *was* gone, but he didn't get far.

Jill turned and spotted him just as Bob was almost inside the office. "Now where do you think you're going?" she called out lightheartedly. "And how did you get out? My goodness, Dr. Greenbriar's right. We *are* going to have to do something about these locks."

Making sure Georgette's door was shut tight, she trotted across the compound and caught Bob by the collar.

"Just what are you snooping around for, huh?" She sat down on a step and began patting him. Bob panted appreciatively.

"Guess it gets kind of lonely out here, doesn't it? It's not like you can talk and keep each other company. Do you miss Tom and Tracy?"

Bob yipped excitedly at the mention of their names.

"I know you do. But they'll be back soon. I don't know why they stopped sending postcards, but I wouldn't worry. I'll bet they miss you just as much as you miss them."

A clock somewhere struck the hour.

"Gosh," Jill said. "I've got to get home. I only stayed late because Georgette's owners had to drop her off tonight and I convinced Dr. Greenbriar he should let me take care of it. He's been working too hard. I worry about him sometimes." She yawned and stretched. "Listen to me ramble on. I'm really tired, aren't you, Bob?"

Bob woofed. Jill smiled at him.

"You're a good dog, Bob," she said. "And I like your hat."

She led him back to his bungalow then, closed the door, checked the latch, and went back inside. As careful as she was, however, she apparently was too tired to remember to cover Ditto's cage—which, as it turned out, was a stroke of good fortune for the rest of us.

No sooner had the light gone out than Ditto began to squawk: *"Oh, what is it again? What is it again? Six-one-one-one-five. Six-one-one-one-five . . . two! That's it, two! That's it, two!"*

"That's it!" another voice echoed.

"My goodness." Georgette's voice floated through the air like a dandelion fluff on a summer breeze. "What all is going on here?"

Whoever had yelled, "That's it!" fell silent.

"Six-one-one-one-five-two?" Chester cried. "That spells *fakeb!* Greenbriar is a *fakeb?*" "Would someone pretty please tell me what's going on?" Georgette said again. "I'm as mixed-up as an acorn on a dogwood tree."

At that, everyone began talking at once. I don't know how she heard anything, but somehow she pulled one name out of all the yammering.

"Hamlet?" she said. "Why, I knew him. I stayed here about a month ago and he was here too. He just left, did you say? Oh, I'm so glad. Archie must've come for him at last. That's all Hamlet was livin' for, y'know."

Before anyone disillusioned her about Archie, Chester thought to ask about someone else.

"Did you know a dog named Rosebud?" he asked.

A hush fell over the place.

"Why, sure," said Georgette. "She and I got to be best friends. And the funny thing is we live right around the block from each other back home. In fact, I just saw her this morning. We had a nice little game of Rip-the-Rag before lunch. Why do you ask?"

"Just curious," said Chester. "What kind of dog is she?"

"A Yorkie."

The next sound I heard was someone panting furiously. Whoever it was sounded terrified. I was less than thrilled to realize it was me.

Chester's door opened as he stepped out into the compound. "There's something I'd like to show you, Georgette," he said.

One by one, all the doors opened. We followed Chester to the familiar mound of dirt in the far corner next to Georgette's bungalow. Chester pawed at the ground until the bones shone in the moonlight. Georgette gasped at the sight, but when Rosebud's collar came into view, she laughed.

"So that's where it went," she said. "That was Rosebud's favorite collar. She lost it one day during a game of Food-Dish-Food-Dish-Who's-Got-the-Food-Dish and we never could find it."

"But it spoke to us," The Weasel said.

"We all heard it," said Bob.

"Those bones, that collar," Linda said.

"She said her name was Rosebud," I explained. "She told us she was a Yorkshire terrier and that she'd been, well . . ."

"Terminated," said Howie. "All because she knew the secret of Chateau Bow-Wow."

"Well," said Georgette with a shrug, "I don't know beans about any secret of Chateau Bow-Wow, but I can tell you this. Rosebud went home weeks ago in the arms of a little girl named Trixie Tucker and she's alive and well. I think y'all are the victims of a hoax."

Chester nodded his head slowly. "I think perhaps we are," he said. He looked around at all of those gathered. Linda averted his gaze, while Bob defiantly stuck out his chin. Felony and Miss Demeanor stared at him with eyes as blank as windows in a house where nobody's home—except you had the feeling somebody was lurking behind the curtains. As for The Weasel, well, he looked so innocent you couldn't help wondering if it was real or just a very good act.

Back in the privacy of our bungalows, I asked Chester, "Who would do such a thing? And why?"

Chester didn't have an answer for me. He just sat, looking out into the dark night, perhaps wondering whether the secret—or the hoax—would reveal itself before the break of day.

EIGHT

Voices in the Night

VOICES again. I had been dreaming about steak tartare, which is really strange because I have no idea what steak tartare is. But it sounded good and I decided I was going to have to have some just as soon as I got home.

My stomach rumbled.

And then I heard the voices again.

"Don't do it for us, do it for Hamlet."

I strained to listen, but all I heard was the click and shuffle of a door opening and the soft rustle of something moving.

"Chester," I whispered.

"Shh."

Chester, apparently, was already awake and listening.

I inched forward to see what I could see. The

moonlight was sufficient to make out three shadowy figures scurrying across the compound. I knew in a flash who they were. Chester knew too.

"Just as I suspected," he said. "The Weasel is nothing but a weasel. And those two cats aren't worthy of the name *Felis catus.*"

What a night. First steak tartare and now this.

" 'Domestic cat,' " Chester explained, anticipating my befuddlement. "I've got to go after them."

"But why? Maybe they're just sneaking inside to watch a little late-night television."

Chester snorted. " 'Don't do it for us, do it for Hamlet.' That's what they said, Harold. It's a conspiracy, don't you see that? What if Hamlet is the ringleader? Greenbriar himself could be involved. Our nation's freedom may be at stake!"

I had the feeling Chester the reader was through with horror novels and had moved on to spy thrillers.

Gingerly, I inquired, "Chester, would you consider the possibility that you might be blowing this thing out of proportion?"

"Not a chance."

"Well, no harm in asking."

In the distance, we heard a soft *beep!* followed by a slightly louder creaking.

"If that's what I think it is . . ." Chester said.

I looked toward the office. The door was wide open.

Suddenly, Ditto squawked, *"Quiet! Do you want to wake everybody up!"*

Chester was out of his bungalow like a hot dog out of a bun with too much mustard.

Howie and I weren't the only ones fast on Chester's heels. In a matter of seconds, Bob and Linda and Georgette had joined us at the office door.

"Stupid bird," we heard someone mutter just inside.

"You may as well give up!" Chester cried. "We've got the place surrounded."

Felony's face appeared at the door. "I shoulda known you'd turn copper," she said to Chester.

In the background, we heard The Weasel crooning, "I'm a poor little weasel who has lost his way."

Chester shook his head.

"It's not what you think," a husky voice said from within. Miss Demeanor sashayed into view. "Come on, Felony, let 'em in. Cute Whiskers thinks he's on to us, huh? Well, what does he know?"

"I know this," said Chester as we filed into the office. I glanced nervously at the long table in the middle of the room. Even without a veterinarian in sight, the thought of that cold steel top was enough to get my hair follicles ready for action. "I know that you three are not on the up-and-up."

"Hah!" Felony retorted. What she lacked in wit she made up in directness. "We told you right out we were cat burglars, didn't we, Miss D.?"

Miss Demeanor nodded.

"Well, we're burglarizing, so there."

"What about him?" Chester said, nodding toward The Weasel, whose eyes were lifted heavenward as his voice segued into another tune, something about "I am Weasel, hear me roar."

"The Weasel?" Felony snorted with contempt.

Hearing his name, The Weasel stopped singing and turned to face us. "I'm innocent," he proclaimed. "They made me do it, honest. They said I'd be helping Hamlet. That's all I wanted to do. I didn't care about the food."

"The food?" Chester's eyebrows arched.

"Okay, okay," said Miss Demeanor. "We may as well come clean. We been trying to break into the food closet to get somethin' decent to eat. You see somethin' wrong with that?"

I looked around. Everyone was nodding approval.

"Is that *all?*" said Chester.

"They weren't going to share!" The Weasel shouted.

Felony turned on him. "Snitch!" she said.

"Well, I can't help it," he went on. "You were going to frame me anyway. That's why I was trying to dig my way out of here. I knew all along what they were up to and I knew they were going to try to get me to take the rap. Just because I'm a weasel."

"Why, you poor thing," said Georgette. "I understand what it's like to be saddled with a reputation you don't deserve. Just because I'm pretty and

sweet and fairly ooze with charm, everyone thinks
I'm stuck-up."

Chester gave Georgette a long look, then turned
back to The Weasel, who had resumed speaking.

"They made me squeeze in through a grate that
leads to the basement. I'm good at squeezing
through small places, you see. And then I punched
in the code to the security system and let them in
the back door."

"Code to the security system?" Chester said
slowly, looking—I say with some pleasure—
confused.

"Six-one-one-one-five-two!" Ditto screaked.

Chester's head dropped.

The Weasel continued his story, apparently relieved to be clearing his conscience of a terrible
burden. "Once they found some good food," he said,
"they were going to *sell* it to everyone else."

Chester lifted his eyes to glare at Felony and
Miss Demeanor. "Why, you're nothing but a couple
of low-life—"

Miss Demeanor batted her eyelashes. "Oh, Cute
Whiskers," she said, "you really know how to
sweet-talk a girl."

"But what about the secret?" Bob asked.

"Or the hoax," said Georgette softly.

"What's Greenbriar's story?" Chester wanted to
know.

"What's become of Hamlet?" Linda asked.

"How much wood would a woodchuck chuck if a woodchuck would chuck wood?" Howie chimed in.

"Quiet, everyone!" Bob said sharply. "What's that?"

We all listened. Somewhere someone was whimpering. We looked to the door at the end of a long, dark hall.

"It's coming from behind that door," Howie said, his eyes growing wide, "the one Rosebud talked about. The one that salted her feet."

"I believe that was 'sealed her fate,' " I said.

"Yeah, that one," said Howie.

"The secret of Chateau Bow-Wow lies behind that door," Chester said.

One after the other, we crept down the dark hallway. The whimpering grew louder. Someone was scratching at the door.

But when we threw the door open . . . there was *no one there!*

I looked around the darkened room and tried to figure out what it was supposed to be. There were chairs and a desk and shelves full of books, but there was also a bed. Howie ran to it and jumped up on his little hind legs. Sniffing at the quilt, he said, "Hamlet has been here."

"And still is," said a disembodied voice.

I don't know about anybody else, but I jumped so high I had a chance to check the wattage in the chandelier.

The door creaked. It began to move. It was clos-

ing, inch by inch, millimeter by merciless millimeter, as it shut us in, trapping us, sealing our fate. My life passed before my eyes. Well, not entirely. I got as far as the time I was a puppy and chewed up Pete's favorite ball, when the door clicked shut.

There in the shadowy corner of the room sat Hamlet, looking scared out of his wits—which, given the state the rest of us were in, should have made him feel right at home.

"I'm sorry," he said, "I didn't mean to frighten you. I just had to make sure you weren't the warden."

The very mention of the word sent Felony and Miss Demeanor into a frenzy. "Euphemistically speaking," he added.

Once Felony and Miss Demeanor had gotten their heart rates back to normal, we all gathered around Hamlet and listened to his version of what had been going on at Chateau Bow-Wow.

He began by giving his head a gentlemanly nod to Georgette. "I'm sorry you had to be involved in this," he told her. "You were always such a lady."

"Oh, Hamlet," Georgette sighed. "What happened? When I heard you were gone, I assumed Archie had come for you at last."

Hamlet rolled his eyes and in so doing revealed two Great Dane—size tears balanced perilously on their rims. One spilled over and landed with a considerable splash on the floor.

"I've known for some time," Hamlet began, "that

Archie was never coming for me. I don't know what's become of him. But I did find out that I was being boarded here out of kindness to Archie's cousin Flo—she and Dr. Greenbriar are friends, it seems—but only until there was no longer a place for me.

"When Harold and Howie and Chester arrived, all the bungalows were filled. I knew I had only a short time in which to escape. However, given the tight security and the fact that my arthritis prevented my digging my own way out, I had no choice but to—well, I hope you'll forgive my saying so— to con others into doing the digging for me."

"Rosebud," said Chester.

"Yes. I found Rosebud's collar and some bones one of the previous guests had left behind and I devised my plan. I would terrify everyone into believing their lives were in danger and that they must work together to escape. Time was crucial, you understand. I only had until the next guest arrived."

Georgette delicately sucked in a tear that had rolled from her eye to the corner of her mouth.

"Oh, it's not your fault," Hamlet told her. "I knew I was on borrowed time. I was just hoping to get an extension on the loan."

"And the secret of Chateau Bow-Wow?" Georgette gently asked.

Hamlet just shook his head. "There is no secret, of course."

Howie looked at Hamlet, confused. "What was going to happen to you once there wasn't a place for you to stay?" he asked.

Hamlet closed his eyes and nodded his head slowly. "I'm afraid I was destined for ... the Big Sleep," he said.

A hush fell over the room. We all knew he wasn't talking about a long nap.

He opened his eyes and continued. "I think Dr. Greenbriar likes me," he said. "He's been keeping me here in his study instead of in one of the kennels down in the basement. But I know it's only a matter of time now."

"Unless," said Chester.

All eyes turned to him.

"Unless we can find Archie."

"But how?" Hamlet asked.

"I'm going to check out your file," Chester answered. "I know my way around the office. I've been inside before. Your file should tell us where Archie is."

"But if he's in Europe—," Hamlet said.

"I doubt that. No, my guess is that he's much closer to home."

And with that Chester exited.

Hamlet regarded us all with sad eyes. "I'm sorry to be so much trouble," he said.

"My goodness," said Georgette, "it seems to me you put yourself through a lot more trouble making up stories about secrets and talking bones than any kind of trouble you could put us through."

"That's what I don't get," said Bob. "Why didn't you just ask us to help you?"

Hamlet sighed. "I'm a useless old mutt," he said. "Nobody wants me anymore. Not Archie. Not his cousin. I couldn't ask, don't you see? What if you had all said no?"

No one had an answer to that. All I could think about was how lucky I was to have the Monroes— and how I couldn't wait to get back home and roll around the living room floor with Toby.

I heard sniffling. Bob said, "There, there, dear, it's all right."

I turned. Linda shook her head sadly as she looked at us looking at her. "It's the kids," she explained. "We haven't heard from them in over a week. It's so unlike them. They said they would write every day. Bob was trying to break out of here in order to find them. What if . . . what if something's happened to them? What if . . . they've left us here and they're never coming back?"

She began to cry. Georgette ran over to her and licked away her tears.

Felony turned to Miss Demeanor. "It's a regular weeporama around here," she said. The fat cat nodded.

"If you don't mind my interruptin' group therapy," Felony said to the rest of us, "I got a question for Hamlet. It's about Rosebud. We all heard her speak. So's what I wanna know is—"

"Oh, that," said Hamlet. If dogs could blush, he would have been blushing. He opened his mouth to explain, but didn't get a word out because Chester suddenly burst into the room.

"I've found Archie!" he cried. "There's only one problem—he's got two addresses. One is here in town. The other's in London."

"London!" Hamlet exclaimed. "I knew it, I knew it! He's playing the palace, sipping tea with the queen, watching the changing of the guard—"

"Excuse me," Chester said. "London is the name of the next town. It's only a couple of miles from Centerville."

"Really?" said Hamlet. He seemed relieved but disappointed at the same time. "Archie always wanted to sip tea with the queen. Ah, well, another time perhaps."

"What're we waiting for?" asked The Weasel. "I've already used the code to disarm the security system here. I'll bet the same code'll work on the gate."

"Now yer talkin' like a weasel!" Felony exclaimed, and I couldn't help noticing The Weasel puff up with pride.

"It'll be daylight soon," Chester remarked as he moved us through the office and out the back door. "Let's get a head start before Dr. Greenbriar and

his assistants show up for work and find us missing."

We were all so excited that no one noticed Ditto watch us file past. No one thought to cover her cage or to tell her not to repeat anything she'd heard.

We were just out the door when Howie said, "Gee, Uncle Harold, this is a real adventure. Hamlet and Archie, together again!"

No one paid attention to the voice that echoed behind us: *"Together again ... Together again! Hamlet and Archie, together again!"*

NINE

Where Is Archie?

IF there was a chill in the early morning air, we didn't notice or mind. All that mattered as we moved single file along the edge of Highway 101 was the importance of our mission. It isn't every day, after all, that six dogs, three cats, and a weasel have the opportunity not only to save one of their own from the Big Sleep, but to bring loved ones together again.

Not that there weren't distractions, mind you.

Dippy Donuts. Bugsy Burgers. Ye Olde Clam-on-a-Roll. Tex-Mex Multiplex. Little Pizza Paradise. It wasn't easy passing one fine dining establishment after another without stopping for breakfast. It's true the restaurants were all closed, but the dumpsters were open. Chester, however, insisted that we keep going, pointing out that we had only a short time before the sun came up. When that happened, we would have to be much more careful about being seen. And being caught.

I knew he was right. But leaving the House of Pies dumpster untouched just about did me in.

"I'll make it up to you, Harold," Hamlet said sympathetically as he limped along beside me. "If we can just find Archie, I'll see to it that he sends you a pie every week for a year. He's rich, you know."

"I didn't know," I said. Not that I was planning on holding Hamlet to his promise, but I will admit just the thought of it helped me get through the next couple of miles.

Luckily for us, Felony and Miss Demeanor knew Centerville like the pads of their filching little paws. As we marched along to the accompaniment of The Weasel's hymn humming, the two cat burglars proudly pointed out their favorite scenes of the crime. They were practically overcome with nostalgia when they realized that the address we were seeking was on the same street as the location of their very first criminal act.

"It was a pastrami sandwich," Felony recalled, her eyes misting over. "Belonged to a guy paintin' a house. Remember, Miss D.?"

"How could I forget?" said the fat, fuzzy one. The way she gazed off into the distance, I expected violins to start playing. "We was practically kittens.

A coupla amateurs. But even then we knew we was destined for great things."

"The way we work is Miss D.'s the good cat, I'm the bad cat," Felony informed us. "She goes in, see, wraps herself around the unsuspecting victim's legs, and purrs up a storm. It don't take long. They pick her up, she nuzzles 'em, and I go in fer the kill."

Miss Demeanor picked up the story. "That's what we did with that painter. He never even knew his pastrami was missin' till he put me down and laid his mitts on a coupla pieces o' rye with mustard and no meat."

They chuckled. "Someday we oughta write a book, Miss D.," said Felony. "What a life we've had."

"You could call it *A Tale of Two Kitties,*" Howie suggested.

"That's not bad," said Miss Demeanor. "Let's see, it could start like this: 'The best of crimes, the worst of crimes . . .' "

Howie yipped enthusiastically while the rest of us shook our heads and Bob and Linda sighed.

Suddenly, Felony cried out, "Hey, that's the street!"

Chester, who had committed both addresses to memory, said, "Treetop Lane. That's it, all right."

It wasn't quite dawn yet, but as we moved slowly down Treetop Lane, the streetlight was enough to make Hamlet realize he'd been there before. He stopped short when we came to the small brick house at the end. There was a name—Cantelloni—on the mailbox.

"Archie isn't here," he said, shaking his head.

"How do you know?" Chester asked.

"Because this is Cousin Flo's. This is where I was staying until . . . that man came along."

We looked at the darkened house as Hamlet continued. "Life was pretty good here for a while. Flo Fenster was a nice lady who never stinted on the dog food. She didn't even get angry when I chewed up one of her favorite slippers. She just said, 'Dogs will be dogs,' and bought herself another pair.

"But one day she met Jed Cantelloni in the produce section of the superette. I was watching through the store window as he approached her with a pineapple in his hand. I saw the look in his eyes when she showed him how to tell if it was ripe. They did the rest of their shopping together and came out of the store all smiles because they'd found out they used the same brand of dish detergent. But he stopped smiling when he saw me. 'Don't you find such a big dog a lot of bother?' he asked her. And she didn't say, 'Oh, no, of course not.' She said, 'He's my cousin's dog.' She never even noticed she'd forgotten to buy my food.

"It was a whirlwind romance. They got married two weeks later and went to Mexico for their honeymoon. On the way to the airport, they dropped

me off at Chateau Bow-Wow. And that's the last I
saw of either of them."

Just then, a light went on in one of the down-
stairs rooms. We all ran to hide behind a bush.
Being the tallest, Hamlet and I were the only ones
who could see inside. Craning my neck, I made out
a man with thinning hair and a thickening middle
scratching his head and yawning. From the way his
lips were moving, it seemed that he was whistling.

"That's him," Hamlet said.

There was a high-pitched yipping.

"And who's that?" I asked.

Hamlet's eyes grew wide. "I don't know," he said.

The front door opened. Out stepped Jed Cantelloni, a jacket thrown over his pajamas. He was
holding a frisky puppy at the end of a leash. "Ready
for our morning walk, Cupcake?" the man who
didn't like dogs said cheerfully. "Let's go then, pal."

"I can't believe it," Hamlet said as they started
down the sidewalk. Cupcake turned briefly and
sniffed in our direction, but fortunately, her master
tugged at her leash and they disappeared around a
corner.

"What an awful person," said Linda, as we
watched them go. "How could he do that to you,
Hamlet?" She shuddered. "This would never happen in Upper Centerville."

"Don't be too sure," said Bob. "We still don't
know what's become of Tom and Tracy."

Bob and Linda gave each other a soulful look.

"How's about we go in and snitch Cupcake's favorite toys?" Felony asked. "Maybe spill her water."

"And we could claw this bum's BarcaLounger while we're at it," Miss Demeanor snarled.

"I appreciate the offer," Hamlet said, "but it isn't the dog's fault, and Cousin Flo, well, she'd be really upset to see any of her furniture ruined, so—"

"But she let this guy get rid of you," said Felony. "Don't you want to get even?"

Hamlet shook his head. "It's not her fault either. It's no one's fault. Why shouldn't they want a cute little puppy instead of an old coot like me?"

"That's enough of that kind of talk," said The Weasel. "Come on, Hamlet, you stick with me. I'm going to cheer you up."

And so, as The Weasel sang "The sun'll come out tomorrow," we set off on the final lap of our journey, the one that would take us to our last hope— the second address in Hamlet's file.

It was daylight now. The streets were getting busy with cars and the sidewalks were filling with people. We were forced to take back roads and, when we could, cut through yards and parks and playgrounds to avoid being too conspicuous. My stomach was making more noise than The Weasel's singing, but we pushed onward, ever onward, knowing that we had little time before we'd be missed and our chance to save Hamlet would be lost forever.

I don't suppose any of us could have anticipated what would lie at our journey's end. Certainly, we never imagined Archie might be living in such a place as the huge stone house that confronted us in the sleepy little town of London.

"Wow," I said to Hamlet when I saw it. "I know you said Archie was rich, but—"

Hamlet looked confused. "He's not *this* rich," he said.

"Well, he sure owns a lot of cars," said Howie. "And, look, he's got servants." Several people in uniform were walking across a yard that was big enough to be a public park.

"Are you *sure* this is the right place?" I asked Chester.

Chester looked up at the address on the gate in front of us: 1717 Burrito Boulevard.

"This is it," he said. "I'm sure of it."

We all looked back at the numbers. That's when we noticed the sign above them. We weren't sure what it meant at first, but Chester explained it to us. Hamlet shook his head sadly.

"What am I going to do now?" he asked.

I lifted my eyes once more and read the words:

SUNNYDALE NURSING HOME

TEN

A Paranormal Experience

WE crept through the gate of the Sunnydale Nursing Home only to be met by another sign. This one was larger than the first and had lots of words written on it, but there were only three that mattered to us at the moment. Three little words near the bottom.

NO ANIMALS ALLOWED.

"Well, Pop," said Howie, "there's your omen."

"More obstacle than omen," Chester muttered. Then, seeing the forlorn look in Hamlet's eyes, he added, "And an obstacle is nothing more than a victory waiting to happen!"

I recognized Chester's statement as one of the many he'd been quoting ever since finishing that recent best-seller, *Everything I Always Wanted to Be I Already Am.* I wondered if The Weasel had read it too; it seemed like his kind of book.

"I appreciate the sentiment," Hamlet said, "but I don't see how—"

"All we need is a plan," Chester said.

Howie ran to a nearby rock garden and pulled a fern out by its roots. "Here," he said, presenting it proudly to Chester.

"That's *plan,* Howie, not *plant.*"

"Oh."

"Keep that up, and we'll be bounced out of here before you can say—"

"Open window."

We all turned at the sound of Felony's voice.

"There's an open window over there by the parking lot," she said. "We make our way under the cars, see; then it's a dash and a leap and we're in."

"Not a bad plan," Chester said, squinting his eyes and nodding approval. "With a little help, it'll be better than not bad. It'll be good."

Felony and Miss Demeanor scowled. I had the feeling they weren't used to having their plans improved upon.

But Chester wasn't used to having somebody else come up with the plan in the first place. "The problem is we don't know what's on the other side of that window," he went on. "Now, the hedge underneath will make an excellent hiding place while one of us gets up on Hamlet's or Harold's back and

checks out the interior. The only other problem is
how we get to the window without being seen."

"I told ya," said Felony, gritting her teeth, "we
skedaddle under the cars."

"But some of us aren't going to fit," Chester
pointed out, with a nod toward Hamlet and me.

"I've got it!" said Howie. "We'll disguise ourselves. That's what they do in the movies. Okay.
It's a nursing home, right? So let's make ourselves
look like nurses. First we need those little white
hats. Wait, I've got a better idea. We could pretend
we're delivering pizza."

"Excellent idea, Howie," said Chester, rolling his
eyes. "Maybe you could write it up and submit it
in triplicate, hmm? Meanwhile, the rest of us will
try to come up with an alternative."

"Okay, Pop," Howie said.

"Let me just give this some thought," Chester
said. "We need to be sure that no one sees Harold
and Hamlet. Hmm."

Hamlet cleared his throat. "If you'll pardon my
saying so, Howie's idea may be useful." Leading
us to a large tree, he indicated a pile of cut-down
branches. "In Shakespeare's play *Macbeth*," he told
us, "an army disguises itself with the branches of
a tree. We could do the same thing. If anyone spots
us, we could just stand still and we'd look like—"

"A bunch of branches with furry feet and tails,"
said Miss Demeanor. "That's the stupidest idea I
ever heard."

"Now, wait a minute," said Chester. "It might just work. After all, a bunch of branches is less likely to raise suspicions than a bunch of animals on the loose."

We nodded our heads. All except Howie, that is, who was too busy trying to figure out what *triplicate* meant.

And so, with branches clenched firmly between our teeth, we set out across the parking lot, looking like a cross between an Arbor Day parade and a very strange family of deer with sprouted antlers. We got close enough to the window so that we could see some movement on the other side when suddenly a door opened and a man and a woman burst out. We froze.

Looking out across the parking lot, the man said, "Listen, Helen, it's all well and good that you want to humor him, but this is a waste of time."

"It may be, George," said the woman. "But he *is* mentally sound. If he said he saw—what was it he said again?"

" 'Birnam Wood come to Dunsinane.' Whatever that means."

"Why, George, it's from Shakespeare. And you know how Archie loves to quote from Shakespeare."

I heard Hamlet gasp. "Archie," he said weakly.

"That's just it," said the man named George. "He loves to quote from Shakespeare. That doesn't mean we have to drop everything and run out here just because he saw a bunch of trees move. He was probably daydreaming about the good old days and—"

The woman placed her hand on the man's arm and he stopped speaking. She pointed in our direction. I gulped and swallowed a little sawdust in the process.

"Look," she said. "Over the roof of the blue Honda. What in the world are those branches doing there?"

The sawdust was tickling my throat. Hamlet, meanwhile, was starting to quiver with excitement from hearing Archie's name. Between the two of us, Birnam Wood was getting a little shaky.

"Good heavens!" the woman cried. "They *are* moving. What is going on?"

The man shook his head. "I don't have a clue," he said. "But there's one way to find out."

With no more warning than that, the two of them moved briskly in our direction. Chester spat out his branch seconds before I sneezed and lost a grip on mine. "Run for it!" he squealed.

"The door!" Felony cried. "They left the door open!"

We ran out from behind the parked cars and scrambled toward the open door before George and Helen knew what was happening.

"Animals!" Helen cried.

"Stop them!" George shouted.

Several residents of the nursing home had gath-

ered on the other side of the open door and instead
of stopping us were cheering us on.

"Look," said a woman with blue cotton candy
hair, "there's a cat that looks just like my Boopsie."

Felony looked up in alarm. "Boopsie?" she said.
"No way do I look like a Boopsie!"

"Boopsie! Here, Boopsie!" the woman called out
after us. We raced madly down a hallway and
through a door into the room with the open window. Hamlet had the lead; so it was that we all
collided with him when he came to a sudden, jar-
ring stop.

"Archie!" he woofed.

Sitting at a table in a tattered bathrobe and
faded pajamas sat an old man with a face full of
whiskers and eyes full of tears. "Hamlet," he said,
opening his arms.

Hamlet limped to him and laid his head on the
old man's knee.

Just then, Helen and George charged into the
room.

"Good heavens!" cried Helen when she saw us.
"Where did all these animals come from?"

"Out!" George yelled, waving his hands in the
air. "Go home! All of you, go home!"

The woman with cotton-candy hair appeared in
the doorway behind them, making clucking noises
with her tongue. "Here, Boopsie!" she said. She
picked up a piece of bacon from one of the tables

and held it out in front of her. "Nice kitty, here, girl."

Felony looked at the rest of us and licked her lips. "Hey, if she wants to call me Boopsie, who'm I to stand in the way of makin' a little ol' blue-haired lady happy?"

Or in the way of a free breakfast, for that matter. "Oh, no, we can't have that," said Helen as Felony (also known as Boopsie) purringly accepted the bacon from the old woman's hand.

The old woman looked up and said, "But they're hungry, Helen." With that, one plate after another found its way from table to floor and we were all treated to a delicious breakfast garnished with pats on the head—even The Weasel, whom one woman said reminded her of the collar of her favorite coat.

Helen and George tried to stop it, but it was no use. The old people were so happy to have us there that the two officials finally threw up their hands and went off to do something official elsewhere.

Hamlet was the only one of us who didn't eat. He was too busy just being with Archie.

"I'm sorry, old boy," Archie said. "I just couldn't bear to tell you the truth. All our travels together, all the thick and thin times, how could I tell you I was leaving you behind for good? Danged nursing home, I don't see what they've got against animals anyway. But this is the only place I could afford, boy. I know, I know, I always said I was rich. And I was. Rich in spirit. But let me confide in you a little secret, dear friend. I've lost my spirit. I'm poor in every sense of the word now, Hamlet. I'm alone. And that's the worst kind of poor there is."

Hamlet cocked his head and whimpered. Archie seemed to know right away what he was saying. "Willie? Oh, Willie and I haven't had a good talk in months. Oh, sure, sure, he's here, but we just don't have anything to talk about anymore."

Hamlet whimpered again.

"You want me to get him?" Archie asked.

Hamlet woofed.

"Really? You want to see Willie?"

The Great Dane panted and woofed some more as Archie's face seemed to grow younger by the minute.

The residents of the nursing home were getting quite a kick out of this exchange.

"Who's this Willie you're talking about?" asked the blue-haired lady, holding—much to my surprise—a purring Felony on her lap. "I don't remember knowing anybody here named Willie."

"You're not talking about William, are you, Archie?" asked a man with thick glasses and an even thicker mustache.

Archie shook his head. "William is a big fellow," he said. "No, no, I'm talking about Little Willie. Why, it's no wonder you've missed him. He's only three feet tall."

I looked at Chester, who had sidled up next to

me. "I think," he commented, "we may have re-united Hamlet with a nut case."

But it was a different kind of case that entered the room moments later—a large suitcase on wheels that was covered with stickers and pulled with considerable effort by Archibald Fenster, the great Shakespearean actor.

Helen and George came in a step behind him to inform us that "someone" was on the way to "see to" the animals. I love hearing things like that. It makes meals sit so easily on the tummy. But they didn't rush out of the room. This time they stayed and, like the rest of us, gathered around Archie to find out what a traveling case on wheels had to do with the mysterious Willie.

"Let . . . me . . . out . . . of . . . here!" a tiny, tinny voice demanded.

It sounded enough like Rosebud to make every hair on my body stand up and salute.

"Are you going to behave?" Archie said to the box.

"Yeah, yeah," said the voice. "Come on, Arch, I been in here for three months. Give me some air, huh?"

Archie looked around the room. Seeing that everyone's eyes were glued to the case on the floor, he bent down and undid the locks.

"Well, it's about *time!*" The voice grew louder as the top opened.

Archie reached in and lifted out . . .

"A dummy!" said Helen, peering over Archie's shoulder. "Why, Archie, you never told us you were a ventriloquist."

"What's a ventriloquist?" Howie asked Chester.

"Ventriloquists," Chester explained, "are people who talk without moving their lips and make it seem as if someone else is doing the talking."

"Like Hamlet and Rosebud," I added.

Hamlet glanced in my direction and nodded bashfully.

"Say, Arch," Willie said. The dummy was now seated on Archie's knee.

"Yeah, Willie?"

"Looks to me like you're losing your hair."

"It's true, Willie. I just don't know what to do about it."

"Yeah, that's a tough decision."

"Tough decision? What do you mean?"

"Toupee or not toupee."

We all laughed. And our laughter encouraged them to go on performing. Archie, I later learned, wasn't really a Shakespearean actor; he just called himself that as part of his act.

"But soft, what light through yonder window breaks?"

"Romeo and Juliet," Chester whispered to me.

"That's no light, Arch," Willie cracked. "That's the sun reflecting off the top o' your head!"

These guys were funny. More than funny, they were good. I guess I should say that Archie was good, since he was doing everything. I had to keep reminding myself that Willie wasn't real.

After an hour or so of watching them perform, I could see that Hamlet had had a good teacher. No wonder he'd had us all convinced those bones could talk.

Just when they were finishing up—"Say goodbye, Willie." "Goodbye, Willie."—I noticed Dr. Greenbriar and Jill standing in the doorway, laughing along with the rest of us. Archie noticed them too. His smiling face grew grim when he saw the words CHATEAU BOW-WOW on Jill's T-shirt.

Putting Willie aside, he stood slowly and said, with quiet dignity, "I suppose you have to take them now."

Dr. Greenbriar nodded. "I'm sorry," he said.

Felony jumped off the lap of the blue-haired lady. "Goodbye, Boopsie," the lady called out sadly.

Another woman removed The Weasel from where she had him wrapped around her neck. "You brought back some happy memories," she told him. "My husband gave me that coat the first year we were married. I wore it to the opera and to the theater. Oh, my, the places we went." She stopped speaking and stroked The Weasel lovingly. And then she let him go.

One by one, we made our way amid gentle touches and soft goodbyes to the door. Only Hamlet remained at his master's side. Archie looked down at him.

"Parting is such sweet sorrow," he said.

Hamlet moaned.

"We've got to do something," Chester whispered to me. "We can't let Greenbriar take Hamlet. You know what it means."

"But what can we do?" I asked.

Chester didn't have an answer right away. And as I watched Hamlet walk slowly toward us and saw Dr. Greenbriar turn to open the door, I couldn't help thinking it was too late.

And then I saw Chester's eyes light up and I heard him say, "How hard can it be to talk without moving your lips?"

He rushed around whispering his plan in all our ears. And a moment later, just as we were about to leave the room for good, the residents of the Sunnydale Nursing Home had a paranormal experience.

The air was suddenly filled with mewing and whimpering and barking. And it couldn't have been us, because our mouths weren't moving at all.

The old people looked around the room, as if it were suddenly flooded with memories.

"Boopsie?" the blue-haired lady said softly. "Is that you?"

The man with the glasses and mustache looked around him. "Sparky? Are you there, boy?"

"Dusty?"

"Whitey?"

"Is that you, Marco?"

"Here, Duke."

"Come on, Lady."

And as the room filled with names, Dr. Greenbriar turned to Helen and George and said, "Rules were made to be broken. Don't you think Sunnydale needs a pet?"

Helen and George looked at each other, then at Archie, who was the only one not calling a name. He was looking into their eyes, asking without any words for Hamlet to be saved.

And they said yes.

Epilogue

THE rest of our week at Chateau Bow-Wow was fairly uneventful. I say "fairly" because everything pales when compared to Rosebud and the emotional reunion of Hamlet and Archie.

Felony and Miss Demeanor were caught trying to break into the food closet the very afternoon we returned from the Sunnydale Nursing Home. And again that evening. And the next morning. And the following afternoon. Where they failed as burglars, however, they did succeed in getting the message across to the management. Our food was finally changed for the better. No more gruel and unusual punishment.

Bob and Linda heard at last from Tom and Tracy—a postcard with a view of a snow-covered mountain. "Dear Bob & Linda," it read, "Have been mountain climbing in quest of tranquillity and the meaning of life. Forgot to bring stamps. Love,

T&T." Bob and Linda celebrated by having a party. They served Nouvelle Lite Lo-Cholesterol Munchies for Your Pet. Chester said he was looking forward to getting home.

The Weasel spent most of his time writing the platform for an animal rights organization he's founding. He's calling it Weasels Into a More Polite Society, or WIMPS for short. I suggested he work on the name.

Georgette and I whiled away the hours playing Rip-the-Rag and reminiscing with Howie about the events leading up to his birth. At first he wanted to hear our stories over and over, but as the week went on he stopped asking for them. Daisy got in the habit of taking him for a walk every afternoon and he told me he enjoyed these strolls much more than the kind down memory lane.

Dr. Greenbriar took the rest of the week off, agreeing with Jill that he'd been working much too hard and needed a vacation.

As for Chester, well, Chester basked in the glory of being a true hero. He also decided he liked ventriloquism, so I had to put up with a lot of talking water dishes, rubber balls, and tree stumps. It wore a little thin after a while, but then Chester came up with a surprise for the Monroes and I have to admit it was worth it just to see the looks on their faces when they arrived to take us home.

"Did you hear that?" Toby said, his mouth hanging open.

"Do it again," said Pete.

Chester winked at me.

"Meow," I said.

"Woof!" said Chester.

The two brothers looked at each other. Mr. and Mrs. Monroe just scratched their heads.

"Perhaps it's something they ate," said Mrs. Monroe. "We'll have to talk to Dr. Greenbriar."

"It's the effects of pollution," said Toby. "Hey, they could be my next science project!"

Pete shook his head. "I think their brains have been taken over by aliens."

Mr. Monroe kept scratching and didn't say a word.

We looked up at them innocently. Howie was laughing so hard he almost gave us away, but the Monroes just thought he was happy to see them.

WE'RE back home now—and happy to be here. It seems we're not the only ones who had an interesting time while the Monroes were away. Kyle's parents reported some strange incidents involving vegetables during Bunnicula's stay at their house. The Monroes apologized but couldn't offer an explanation.

Chester just shook his head. "When are those people going to realize their precious little bunny is a vampire?" he said to Howie and me.

"A vampire?" Howie said. He lifted his chin and

let out an ear-piercing howl. *"Ahoooooooooo!"* Chester sighed. I smiled.

A dachshund who howls like a werewolf.

A vampire rabbit.

A dog who meows and a cat who barks.

Things were definitely back to paranormal.